10662727

Toy Trouble

More **Strange Matter**™ from
Marty M. Engle & Johnny Ray Barnes, Jr.

No Substitutions

The Midnight Game

Driven to Death

A Place to Hide

The Last One In

Bad Circuits

Fly the Unfriendly Skies

Frozen Dinners

Deadly Delivery

Knightmare

Something Rotten

Dead On Its Tracks

Plant People

Toy Trouble

Marty M. Engle

A
MONTAGE
PUBLICATION

Montage Publications, a Front Line company,
San Diego, California

If you purchased this book without a cover, you should be aware that this book is stolen property. It was reported as "unsold and destroyed" to the publisher, and neither the author nor the publisher has received any payment for this "stripped book".

No part of this publication may be reproduced in whole or in part, or stored in a retrieval system, or transmitted in any form or by any means, electronic, mechanical, photocopying, recording, or otherwise, without written permission of the publisher. For information regarding permission, write to Front Line Art Publishing, 9808 Waples Street, San Diego, California 92121

ISBN 1-56714-052-1

Copyright © 1996 by Front Line Art Publishing. All rights reserved. Published by Montage Publications. Montage Publications is a division of Front Line Art Publishing.

Printed in the U.S.A.

**TO OUR FAMILIES
&
FRIENDS**
(You know who you are.)

1

"Clear the way! Clear the way! Car crash victim coming through!" I yelled through the paper dust mask fixed tightly over my nose and mouth. "A beautiful young woman's life is in our hands!" Already I could feel the adrenaline rushing through me, and the familiar pounding in my chest.

I pushed her along the carpet toward the waiting operating area.

"Pupils fixed and dilated," I muttered, staring down at the victim's perfect face. Her blue eyes stared up at me, unblinking. I could feel them staring into me, trusting me with her very life. I would not fail her. I *could* not fail her as I had failed the others.

I'm Karen Sanders, 11 years old. As Chief Surgeon of the ER, I see a lot of tragic cases pass through these doors, but this had to be one of the worst.

"What's the story on this one?" Nurse Fuzzy Bear asked, moving swiftly to the operating table.

"Slammed by a pink convertible in front of her dream house. Get me a crash cart and one of those electro-cardio thingies with all the monitors and dials! NOW!"

Instantly, Nurse Fuzzy Bear and her friends shoved the hi-tech medical equipment to the operating table.

"HEY!" I yelled, catching Blueberry Muffin's™ attention. "Do you consider a berry-scented dress with a big, floppy hat a standard nurse's uniform?"

She hung her large head in shame.

"No time for you to change into something more appropriate! Get the electro-paddle shockers, NOW!" I demanded.

Big Jake™ moved silently up beside me, ready to move the victim from the roller-cart thing to the operating table. His bare, muscular arms reached down and . . .

"DON'T MOVE HER HEAD!" I cried, warning him. "She may have a fractured neck or something! ON THREE! One . . . two . . . three . . . GO!"

Big Jake™, Nurse Fuzzy Bear, and I moved the poor woman to the operating table. Her whole body seemed stiff as a board. Her long, blonde hair seemed unnaturally wiry.

Wasting no time, I pulled the desk lamp over her face. My top-flight surgical team went to work.

"Plastic tubing. NOW!" I yelled.

Nurse Fuzzy Bear finished taping the tubes to both of the victim's arms. "Arms and legs stiff and skinny! No noticeable joints!"

"Just as I suspected," I mumbled, pushing my finger against her head, feeling it wobble back and forth. "The free-rolling ball joint is coming loose." My heart sank. I'd seen this before.

"FLAT LINE!" Nurse Blueberry Muffin™ called from the electro-cart thing.

"CLEAR!" I yelled.

Instantly, my crew fell away from the operating table as I plunged the foam paddles with their curly cords down onto the victim's chest, hoping the shock would bring her back.

I pressed my ear down to her chest.

Nothing!

"CLEAR," I yelled again.

The crew glanced nervously at each other. They knew I wouldn't give up, not even when it was too late. They didn't say a word, just stared at each other with glassy eyes.

I pressed my ear down to her chest.

Nothing.

"C'mon! Don't give up on me now! You have too much to live for! Think of your vast wardrobe, your dream house, your long, stylable hair! FIGHT! FIGHT!" I cried, plunging the foam paddles down onto her again.

"WE HAVE A HEARTBEAT! You did it, Dr. Sanders," Blueberry Muffin™ gasped, never taking her eyes from her monitor.

The crew breathed a sigh of relief.

Then the victim's head fell off!

"NO!" I gasped. "QUICK! NURSE FUZZY BEAR! STICK THAT BACK ON!"

The crew panicked, scrambling for even more expensive equipment.

"The head's no good," Nurse Fuzzy Bear cried, inspecting the hollow interior.

"Big Jake™! Replacement head! Hurry! We're losing time!" I yelled.

4

Quickly, he and I rummaged through the shoebox full of replacement heads. Mostly blondes. A redhead. Nothing quite . . . Hmmm.

Decisions like these are why I'm the head surgeon. The incredible pressure and mind-numbing stress have destroyed lesser surgeons. But not me, Karen Sanders, M.D.

I made my decision.

"Hollow or not, that head's going back on! Super-glue. NOW!" I cried, as gasps and applause erupted from the crew.

I popped the top off the tube of Super-glue and squeezed out a drop onto the rounded stump of the neck.

"Such finesse," Nurse Fuzzy Bear remarked.

"That's why I'm head honcho," I muttered, finishing the job. The head fit back on perfectly, *but would it stay?* I winced as I remembered the ones that hadn't.

"Keep an eye on her vitals," I said, pulling my mask off, sighing, and rubbing my forehead. "I'll tell ya', Nurse Fuzzy Bear. This is the part I hate . . . talking to the boyfriend."

With head bowed, I approached the boyfriend, seated stiffly on the floor. *What a brave man,* I thought to myself. Despite the incredible strain he must be feeling, his hair was perfect and his mouth was fixed in a wide smile.

"The truth, doctor. Please. Will she make it?" he asked, disguising the fear that must have been tearing him apart inside.

Sheepishly, I looked down and said quietly, "One moment . . ."

I quickly grabbed my eight ball and started shaking it, thinking to myself, "Will SunFun Darcy™ live?"

I turned the eight ball over and gazed down at the little round window, licking my lips, anxiously awaiting the answer.

Tragedy or triumph?

The little triangle came into view, fuzzy in the blue liquid, bouncing slightly . . . then the answer—**Ask again later.**

With every ounce of strength and poise I could muster, I turned to the boyfriend.

"It's too early to be certain. I . . ."

Then my bedroom door opened and a tall, dark figure stepped through.

I gasped, staring up from the floor, surrounded by my dolls spread all around the shoebox operating table in front of the bed.

The weary figure glared at me, eyes narrowing, struggling with an arm-load of freshly cleaned clothes.

"Hi, Mom," I muttered, hanging my head. *Caught!* Caught *playing* with my toy collection. How embarrassing.

Mom huffed, stepping over the scattered, shattered remains of tonight's many ER patients. "Karen Sanders. What have I told you? If you don't stop wrecking your toys, they're going to wreck you!"

"Give me a break, Mom," I huffed, jumping to my feet. "This SunFun Darcy™ isn't worth anything. A $1.99 bargain bin special at Toys Galore. She doesn't even have accessories."

Mom shook her head at the towering stacks of fashion dolls on my dresser as she began putting my clothes away. "Well, that's a perfectly good Blueberry Muffin™ lying on the floor."

"Oh, I have three more still in their packages in my collector's case. This one's to play with." The berry-scented figure squeaked as I kicked it under the bed.

"I think you should get rid of at least half of these toys," Mom grumbled, turning the light on in my closet.

She yelped, startled by a hundred stuffed

animals staring out with plastic eyes.

"OH, MY—KAREN? Where did these come from?"

"Natalie. She . . ."

Mom raised her hand. "Enough. This is getting way out of hand. We're going to have to build a new wing onto the house if you accumulate any more. Time for a yard sale."

"Yeah, right! As if! If I keep going, this collection will be so famous, I'll have to open a museum because of public demand. I'll be rich beyond my wildest dreams and I'll do nothing but roam the world, seeking out new and more unusual toys for the internationally renowned 'Sanders Toy Exhibition'."

"Well, I won't quit my day job just yet." Mom sighed, accidentally stepping on Big-Jake™, squishing his vinyl face into a pucker. "Honestly, Karen. Pick up your casualties before bed, all right? Are you and Jill still going to that new toy shop tomorrow?"

"You bet. We've been waiting all week. Natalie's going, too."

Mom moaned and shook her head at the mention of Natalie's name. "Be sure to take Calvin with you. He wants to go, too."

"He wants to go because Natalie's going. That's the only reason," I replied, laughing.

Mom doesn't like Natalie much. She calls her the princess of excess. Natalie gets anything she wants, and lots of it. Mom does like Jill, however. Jill is my other best friend and has a doll collection that puts mine to shame. She has about a hundred dolls, mostly porcelain, each with its own stand. Even though she doesn't have quite as many as Natalie, she takes better care of them.

We all live in the same subdivision of Fairfield, Asbury Estates, so we get to see each other all the time. Too much of the time, Mom says.

Mom finished putting my clothes away and paused at the bedroom door. "This time, Karen, let Calvin get what *he* wants with his allowance. No scheming."

"No prob," I said as innocently as I could. I could talk my little brother, Calvin, into anything. A lot of times I'd convince him to pool our money to get stuff I couldn't afford alone.

"Get to bed soon, okay?"

I nodded as Mom closed the door behind her. Swiftly I grabbed the eight ball and plopped onto the bed. How other people live without an eight ball is beyond me. It's almost always right. I don't even think about making a decision without consulting with the eight ball first. Besides, who can resist a little sneak-peek at the future?

"Will I find something incredible tomorrow at the toy store that will change my life forever?"

I watched the plastic triangle bounce and bob and float to the top.

YES.

"Cool."

Then I thought of Mom's harsh warning and the stern look on her face.

I shook the eight ball again. "Will I get in trouble for it? Am I in for some serious toy trouble?"

The triangle bobbed to the top.

IT IS CERTAIN.

3

I could feel the excitement grow inside me as I pedalled faster and faster. Then, I slowed my bike and drifted into the parking lot of Fairfield Village Square, a renovated strip mall across from a big office complex.

The parking lot was nearly empty, with only a few cars parked in front of a brand-new bagel shop. Further down the row of shops are an ice cream parlor, a dentist's office, and in the largest building, the brand-new Kepler's Toys and Collectibles.

I coasted to a stop. The crisp Saturday morning air filled my lungs as I breathed in deeply and sighed. Soon my collection would grow, thereby securing my future. "Ahh." Nothing could beat the excitement of a new, unexplored toy store. I could hardly wait to see if the eight ball's prediction would come true. I pushed forward and began pedalling faster than before, zooming across the parking lot.

The store fronts whizzed by as Kepler's Toys and Collectibles grew closer.

The first thing I noticed was the remarkable size of the place. It looked as large as a theatre, like an eight-screen multi-plex or something.

The bright blue letters above the glass doors were the type that would light up at night. Expensive-looking. Not a mom-and-pop type place. It looked like a major chain, though I had never heard of Kepler's before.

"Promising," I mumbled. I could judge from the look of the place that I would find mostly ordinary toys; mass-produced, overexposed power ninjas and their cousins. Still, the "collectible" part of the name meant they had to have at least a *few* unusual toys.

Then I noticed Jill and Natalie waving, standing near the bike rack by the door. Jill was wearing a white sweat shirt and plain jeans, looking like one should look on a Saturday morning. Like she woke up, put on something resembling clothes, and walked out the door.

Natalie looked like an oversized SunFun

Darcy™; short, black skirt, black tights, yellow top with black polka dots, and curly blonde hair topped with a black bow.

Jill already had that exhausted look on her face, the kind from being around Natalie too long. Don't get me wrong. Natalie's a good friend, but she can grate on your nerves after awhile. She simply doesn't think before she speaks, and her favorite topic is herself.

I pulled my bike into the rack as they greeted me with eager smiles.

"KAREN! Glad you're here," Jill sighed in relief. "The doors are open and we're the first ones here!"

Natalie stepped toward me and whispered, "I'm afraid this shop isn't quite as large as I wanted it to be. Still, maybe we can find something to make it worth the trip."

Jill rolled her eyes behind Natalie's back, as usual, forcing me to laugh.

"My eight ball said I would find some great stuff today, guaranteed," I smiled.

"What are we waiting for?" Jill laughed.

"What else?" I groaned.

"ME!" Calvin whined, pedalling as fast as he could to catch up. Calvin's four-foot nothing frame wasn't built for speed. He's kind of round and blustery and wears clothes three sizes too large. He has a crush on Natalie, though he would never admit it in a million years. Like most fourth grade boys, he pretends to loathe all girls. Still, Natalie is the only person he will tuck his shirt in for. A sign of true love.

"Hurry up, Calvin! I'm sick of waiting for you," I yelled.

The girls cooed and teased as Calvin finally pulled into the bike rack, breathing heavily. "Hey, babe. I'm *worth* waiting for."

"Calvin, for heaven's sake, tuck your shirt in!" Natalie quipped.

Calvin grumpily complied, shoving his flannel shirt sloppily into his jeans.

"Do you have plenty of cash, bro?" I asked, smiling.

Calvin stepped back defensively. "Yes. Yes, I do. *I* have plenty of money. For me."

"Let's go, brother dear. I'll even hold the door."

"Howdy, folks! Welcome to Kepler's Toys and Collectibles! The happiest store for kids of all ages!" The large brachiosaur's head swung down to meet us. The mouth moved in perfect time to the prerecorded message. Its eyes blinked. Its long neck swayed through the air, pointing to a painted jungle on the store wall.

"Cool way to greet people!" Jill exclaimed.

Natalie pushed rudely past her to secure a better view, coming within inches of the large dino's nose. "Not quite as advanced as Disneyland, but adequate."

Then I noticed the well.

It was like a cartoon wishing well, large and on a low platform in the front of the store. Stuffed toys of all types were piled around it. Colored spotlights revealed a big cartoon bucket and rope, and a large crank on the side of the well wall. A sleeping cartoon face poked out from its stony front.

As we approached, the cartoon face opened its eyes and began to laugh. "You'll find delights and surprises on every aisle. If you have any questions, don't hesitate to ask any of our friendly staff. Enjoy your visit!"

Overhead, mechanical monkeys rode unicycles on high wires. Bright yellow planes sailed in circles on the end of their wires. Flashing neon lights stretched across the ceilings and along the walls.

"This is the most awesome store I've ever seen!" Jill exclaimed.

"Yeah. This *is* pretty cool," I said, trying to take it all in. "Stay close, Calvin."

Calvin was already hunched over, counting his money and looking around nervously.

We wandered down aisle after aisle. At first we tried to stay together, but, as usual, we ended up drifting to the areas that we were most interested in.

Jill gazed dreamily at the porcelain dolls, displayed in rotating glass cases, each with beautiful clothing and hair.

Natalie sashayed down the Darcy™ aisle, peering down her nose at the symbols of excess that only someone as popular, pretty, and impossibly shaped as Darcy™ could enjoy. Pink sports cars, pink dream homes, pink wardrobes, and pink pets.

Calvin ran from action figure line to action figure line, deciding on who could fight whom (within scale) and who would fit inside the majority of the paramilitary vehicles he already had.

As for me, try as I might, I couldn't find anything I hadn't seen before. Talking parrots that record your voice and play it back. Life-size dolls. Plastic pets that would fit in your pocket, and so on, but not one single thing I hadn't expected. Nothing to further the great 'Sanders Toy Exhibition'.

"Having some toy trouble, young lady?" a voice cackled, startling me.

Toy trouble. Who? How?

The voice came from the top of a ladder that towered beside me. A strange old man was at the top, placing a cardboard box carefully on the shelf.

"Can't find that something special, eh?" he laughed. "You're looking for a one-of-a-kind. I can tell." He chuckled as he slid down the ladder and landed in front of me.

He stood about five feet tall. No hair, except for a little tuft of gray over the ears. His glasses were as thick as bottles and sat perched on the end of his nose. His baggy features reminded me of the brachiosaur's that had greeted us at the door. He had a yellow shirt with a brown vest that was frayed at the edges.

"I-I'm looking for something unusual for

my collection," I managed to stammer, watching him lean closer to get a better look at me. His eyes seemed greatly magnified through his glasses, though his pupils looked like pinholes. He blinked a couple of times and straightened his back.

"Ah, my dear. I can tell you are tired of transforming ninja-robot teenagers, ridiculously proportioned heroes in candy-colored costumes, and dopey-eyed gimmick dolls that grow tiresome within an hour of play. Heads that snap off. Capes and shoes that vanish without a trace. Stupid, little accessories that wind up in a vacuum cleaner bag. Am I right? Hmmm?"

I nodded.

"I understand. We have a lot in common, you see. You, like I, seek a finer collectible. Something not quite so common, so run-of-the-mill, so ordinary. My name is Francis Kepler," he said with a bow.

Kepler. Of Kepler's Toys and Collectibles. Wow.

"You are?"

"Karen. Karen Sanders."

He signalled for me to follow him through a door in the back of the shop I hadn't noticed before, right beside the swinging doors that led to the warehouse. A sign on the door read:

Under Construction

"Well, follow me, Karen Sanders. I have a treat in store for you." His eyes gleamed as if he had the most incredible secret in the world.

"I have something, I guarantee, you will not be able to live without."

4

The room behind the door, as near as I could tell, seemed to be an unfinished toy museum; large glass cases, track lighting, plush rugs on a hardwood floor. The muted colors of antique toys gleamed under the shafts of light in the few displays that were finished. *A museum like the one I would open.* For a moment I felt angry at Mr. Kepler. Then I felt his soft hand on my shoulder and the anger fled away.

"You'll be my first customer, Ms. Sanders. My special, first customer." The old man seemed to be talking to the room more than to me. His head turned slowly and his eyes appeared to drift around in the thick glasses he wore on his face. "Please, look around."

I found myself instinctively moving forward, awestruck, gazing from case to case. It was as if he knew exactly what I would have done and built it before I ever had the chance. I couldn't decide between crushing disappointment or gleeful excitement.

In the cases lay the toys I never knew I wanted, but could now not live without.

"Th-They're wonderful," I stammered, though the words couldn't match the emotion.

My fingers danced over the case containing an ancient-looking miniature carousel, crafted with a level of detail I had never seen in a toy. The jewels and mirrors caught the light from above beautifully.

A dark-brown felt bear with large black eyes and a shiny black nose greeted me next. He smiled at me with a charm lacking in his pastel-colored brothers that crowded the wire bins in the front of the store.

Then I saw him. *The one I had to have.* My heart beat faster as my hands pressed against the case. Love at first sight.

A jester doll.

His lumpy soft body was crafted from a cream and dark-red diamond-patterned cloth. A silky hat, topped with a brass bell, drooped in front of his white porcelain face. His eyes shone bright and white, like two pearls. His mouth upturned in a smile, a shallow carving beneath his long, pointed nose.

I could not tear my eyes away from him. He seemed to be staring straight at me, sitting awkwardly in the case.

"Nice isn't he? But don't for a moment think I've nothing but old fuddy-duddy toys. No ma'am. Quality doesn't mean old-fashioned. I have my own line of powerful heroes in perfect detail, starships you would swear could actually function. Every toy you could imagine and more. Designed and built by Francis Kepler." He merrily pointed and waved at the toys in the cases all around, some in cardboard boxes, some still wrapped in newspapers, others in white cloth.

The all-important question came to mind, causing sweat to break on my face. "How much do they cost?" I asked, bracing myself for the worst.

He stepped closer and told me.

Excitedly, I sprinted down the action figure aisle in the main store, my brother still comparing the pros and cons of the Star Warriors™ line to Amazin' Changin' Power Fighters™.

"C'mon! Calvin, c'mon! Right now! There's something I have to show you!" I pulled him by the sleeve, down the aisle toward the unfinished exhibit room.

His sneakers squeaked against the floor. "Stop! No way! Not this time. No way are you going to con me out of my meager allowance. I don't care WHAT you've found."

"Calvin. CALVIN! Trust me. You won't believe your eyes."

After gathering Jill and Natalie, the four of us got a grand tour of Kepler's unfinished toy museum.

The old man loved toys even more than we did. No matter what toy question we could think of, he had an answer for it.

He won Calvin's love and admiration for winning the debate between the pros and cons of Microbotics™ action figures and Cyber-Rangers™.

He showed us almost every toy that he had, and even designs for some he hadn't built yet.

The only things he wouldn't show us were the contents of two, big, unopened crates, one leaning on an empty case, the other lying on the floor of the museum.

Above them I noticed a blind-covered window. The blinds were turned open and through them I could see the warehouse, hundreds of thousands of crates and boxes . . . all filled with toys.

Without a doubt, we all agreed it was the best Saturday we'd ever had.

The best part? We went home with some of his special toys.

Calvin bought an incredibly complex starship with lights and sounds.

Jill bought the most beautiful dolls in her collection so far.

Natalie bought a special limited edition fashion doll that surpassed even SunFun Darcy™.

As for me, I bought the jester . . . and the bear, too.

I felt slightly guilty because we paid less for Kepler's toys than we would have for the big-name toys. He said as his first and most special customers, we were entitled to a special discount . . . as long as we told all our friends. Of course, we agreed.

As we left the store to retrieve our bikes

for the ride home, other kids and parents began to arrive. I had to smile as I watched the anxious little kids pulling their mothers and fathers through the automatic glass doors, their minds on the common, everyday, run-of-the-mill stuff they could find almost anywhere.

Somehow, I knew that we were special. That Mr. Kepler wouldn't show anyone else the unfinished toy museum. That we were the only people who would see them for now.

As I stared at my new, one-of-a-kind prize, the jester doll, I couldn't help but think that I was the luckiest girl in the world. The eight ball was right. I found the toy I could not possibly live without.

It wasn't until that night I realized I wasn't so lucky after all.

Maybe I found the toy I could not possibly live *with*.

SATURDAY 9:45pm

I cautiously opened the door to Calvin's room. I had to check on him before I went to bed, to make sure he was asleep. A nightly precaution because Calvin loves playing practical jokes on me.

Captain Calvin was already asleep, tired from flying his Kepler starship in raids against the evil Insectors™ and their armies of drones. His body was sprawled amongst the bedsheet canyons and cliffs of the planet.

Calvin's bed was always 'the planet', whichever planet the Insectors™ lived on. The carpet would either be a vast alien ocean or a pit full of acid waiting for the bad guys to fall in, depending on his mood.

I watched for unusual movement. Any sign of faking. None that I could see. I was safe enough, I supposed.

Entering my room, I carefully placed my new jester doll on the chair near my door.

His head slumped to the side and I had to scoot him up a couple of times as his soft, lumpy body slid down against the slick wooden back. I finally got him to stay. "There you go," I muttered before heading to the bathroom.

The floor was littered with toys and dolls that Natalie, Jill, and I had played with after our return from Kepler's.

I prepared for bed like usual. Brushed my teeth, brushed my hair, washed my face, picked out some clothes for Sunday, and tossed Fuzzy Bear onto the bed. Miss Bear is my usual sleep partner because she collapses very easily. Over the years, I have pressed her nearly flat.

I had already put my new Kepler bear away in the closet.

The jester doll watched me as I picked up the rest; Blueberry Muffin™, Big Jake™, SunFun Darcy™, and all the others, finally placing them in the toy box by the window.

I walked back over and kneeled down one

more time to look at the jester's face. I didn't want to touch him again because he was so hard to get to stay up.

His eyes stared into space, gleaming like two small pearls. His cheeks had a faint rosy cast, painted at each upturned end of his carved mouth. I carefully tapped the bell at the end of his hat and listened to the soft jingle.

I flipped the overhead light switch off, leaving only the glow from the lamp on my bedstand.

"Good night, Mr. Jester," I said, springing into bed and reaching for the lamp on my bedstand. I stopped as my fingers found the switch. "OH! I almost forgot."

I left the light on and reached for my eight ball. "Will tomorrow be as great as today was?" I shook the ball vigorously.

The triangle bounced and floated to the top of the window—**No. Definitely not.**

"Oh, that's just great. Will I be miserably unhappy?"

The triangle turned and bobbed in the little window—**Yes.**

I felt my heart sink and my stomach go hollow. I knew I shouldn't take the eight ball so seriously . . . but it was usually right.

I steadied myself and licked my lips, shaking the eight ball again. "Am . . . am I going to be in danger?"

The triangle bounced and floated to the top of the window—**It is certain.**

I dropped the eight ball to the floor with a gasp and heard it roll under the bed. "Get a grip, Karen. It's just a stupid eight ball."

I turned and looked at the shadowy figure of the jester, staring at me from the chair by the door. Even in the dark I could see his pale, pearly eyes staring at me, smiling. They didn't seem quite as pleasant as before. I couldn't be sure if it was my imagination, but I would have sworn his smile changed.

"G-Good night," I said, then flipped off the light.

The jester's eyes glowed red through the dark, staring straight at me.

I SCREAMED! Shrieking, I clutched at the covers, feeling my heart explode in white bursts of terror, unable to believe what I saw.

The light flipped on and Mom came running into the room. "KAREN! KAREN! What's wrong? What is it?"

I couldn't breathe. I couldn't speak. I sobbed in great gasps, pointing frantically toward the jester doll with a pale, trembling hand.

Mom roughly picked up the jester doll and held it like a rag. The limp body draped over her hand as his hat swung down, pointing at the floor. His eyes were the same pearly white they were only moments before.

"The doll, sweetheart? What is it? What about the doll?" Mom asked, rushing over with the jester in her hands.

"Its eyes. Its eyes. They glow!" I screamed, kicking at the sheets, scooting away from the figure as Mom sat on the bed.

"It's just a doll, sweetheart. Oh, I knew it. This thing is too creepy looking. Just like I said at dinner. It gave you a bad dream."

I quieted down, controlling my sobs, staring at the limp, helpless figure in Mom's hand. *It's just a doll. A stupid doll.*

Sense started to flood back into my system. Maybe I did dream it or imagine it. I felt like a total idiot now. Either the eight ball had spooked me or I'd spooked myself.

"Well, if you're going to keep this thing,

put it away at night. Okay? So it doesn't give you bad dreams. All right?" Mom said.

As she headed for the door, I called after her. "Mom, will you put him in the living room or something, just for tonight? I'll find a case or a stand for him tomorrow."

"Sure," Mom sighed, flipping off the light. The jester stared at me, hanging upside down in Mom's hand, as the door closed silently behind her.

I drifted back to sleep, clutching my sheets tightly.

SUNDAY 12:45am

A shuffling sound woke me suddenly.

My eyes grew wide and my heart began pounding as I strained to listen in the darkness of my room. *A shuffle.*

I didn't move a muscle. I didn't even lift my head. I didn't dare. I swallowed hard and listened, my eyes darting in the darkness. I tried to stop the images of walking dolls that formed in my mind.

Someone was awake and walking around—but not in my room. Not loud enough for that. No. Definitely somewhere else in the house. The kitchen, maybe? The hall?

The living room?

I heard another small, soft shuffle.

Then a creak.

My door opening?

"No," I whispered. My heart began to pound harder. My breath became more shallow. No, not the door opening. More like footsteps on the floor.

The creak again.

I held my breath and felt the first tear squeeze from my eye and run down my cheek.

"Get a grip, Karen. Don't let your imagination run away with you. As if some lame, homicidal doll is coming to kill you. That only happens in the movies. Not in real life. Just calm down . . ."

A creak sounded right outside my bedroom door.

I tried to control my breathing, fighting back the waves of panic that nearly paralyzed me where I lay. I lifted my head from my covers, even though I didn't want to, and forced myself to look at the door.

The light was on in the hallway.

I could see the light coming through the crack at the bottom of the door.

Then I noticed two slender shadows through the crack, moving ever so slightly in the hallway.

Legs! My brain screamed. Terror shot through my body, sending me into shivers. Someone was standing just outside my bedroom door.

My mouth opened to call out to Mom, or to whomever was on the other side of the door.

Then it occurred to me.

"Calvin," I snarled. It would be just like him to pull a stunt like that about now. "Well, not this time, rat face." I eased from the bed and crept toward the door.

I was halfway to the door when the shadows stopped moving. Whomever was there, was waiting right outside the door, *practically in the door frame.*

I growled at the thought of my little brother standing there, waiting to get me.

I reached for the doorknob.

"Hope you're ready for a shock, little man," I growled.

With a swift jerk, I pulled the door open

34

and found . . .

Cold dread swept over me. I looked down and SCREAMED!

The jester doll stared up at me, standing in the door frame, a gleaming kitchen knife in his hand, a broad smile on his face.

I fell backward, screaming and clawing at the air, waiting, dreading the attack. The weight of the little figure on my stomach. The terrible sight of his cloth arms raising high over his head, a silvery gleam in his porcelain hands.

Then I heard the laughter. A little boy's laughter. Calvin's laugher.

He laughed so hard, he rolled onto the hallway floor right behind the jester doll, still standing stiffly and stupidly in the door frame.

"CALVIN! I CAN'T BELIEVE YOU!" I yelled at the top of my lungs.

"I'm s-sorry," Calvin laughed, wiping a tear from his eye. "I overheard you earlier and couldn't resist." He continued laughing and pulled at the butter knife he had taped to the jester's hand, nudging the wire doll-stand holding the jester upright. "Y-You should have seen yourself. Oh, man. Priceless! THE DOLL! THE DOLL! Ha, ha, ha," Calvin laughed.

"You nearly gave me a coronary, you little creep! I ought to stuff you down the sink!" I yelled, as Mom came down the hall, clutching her robe shut.

"What is going on . . . all right, Calvin. Joke's over. If you're not in bed by the time I count to three, you are . . ."

Calvin flew down the hall and into his room, jerking the door shut behind him, laughing all the while.

"Can you believe this? Can you believe what he did to me? I hope you're going to chain him up now! He shouldn't be allowed to leave his room, EVER!" I cried.

"I'll deal with Calvin tomorrow. Go on to bed," Mom said, leaning over to pick the jester up from the floor.

"Wait a minute. I'll keep the doll in *my* room, Mom," I said, beating her to it and lifting the jester from the floor. "I don't want it to fall into Calvin's hands again."

"You sure? You sure it won't give you bad dreams?" Mom asked.

"Nah. I must have been half-asleep before. Or had a stupid-attack. Don't worry about it. If he comes to life anymore tonight, I'll sic him on Calvin."

"Good night, Karen." Mom sighed, then went back down the hall. Her bedroom door closed with a click.

SUNDAY 1:12am

After a glass of cold milk in the company of Mr. Jester, I decided to forget Calvin's little prank and go back to bed. I would come up with some kind of revenge scheme, a fiendish joke to make the little brat squirm, but it would have to wait. I could barely keep my eyes open, in spite of the earlier excitement. I grabbed Mr. Jester from where he sat on the kitchen table and headed back to my room.

I placed the jester doll on the night stand by the bed, letting him slump against the lamp, the only light on in the bedroom.

I plodded past the bed into the bathroom to wet my face, flipping on the light, and turning the faucet on with a sigh.

I splashed some cool water on my face,

then glanced up into the mirror, staring through the opened bathroom door into the bedroom.

I saw the jester, flopped awkwardly on his side, his hat shining brightly under the lamp. He seemed almost comical. Laughable, like a clown. I smiled as the water dripped from my face. I couldn't believe that I was actually afraid of a doll.

Then my heart exploded into bursts of panic as I watched the doll in the mirror twitch, jerk . . . *and stand up.*

The jester *stood up* on the night stand, scrambling swiftly to his feet. His limp body became rigid as his arms swayed in the air.

My eyes were locked onto his hideous animated body. My stomach lurched and heaved at the sight.

He reached under the lampshade with the sureness of someone *used* to movement, of someone moving with a purpose. *He's done this before,* I remember thinking to myself, nearly laughing in disbelief.

"No. Please. It can't be. IT'S IMPOSSIBLE!" I gasped.

He stared at me then. He snapped his head up and stared at me with glowing red eyes, his arm held out stiffly from his side.

He turned out the light.

Darkness swallowed the bedroom. Complete and utter blackness of an unnatural sort. The light from the bathroom wasn't penetrating the gloom of the bedroom the way it should. It stopped at the doorway as if hitting a wall, making the bathroom seem all the more bright.

I peered into the mirror with wide eyes, terrorized beyond movement. Water dripped from my face, or was it sweat? I couldn't tell. I couldn't turn my head or even cut off the steadily running faucet. I knew somewhere in the darkness a hideous little doll waited.

Crouched by the bed?

Hiding by the door?

Maybe grinning on my pillow.

I carefully reached behind me with my foot, catching the edge of the bathroom door, trying to keep from screaming. *Do I have time to close the door? Does he see me?*

Then I heard a thud in the darkness, like a soft sack dropping to the floor.

I slammed the bathroom door shut with a

kick, spun around, hurtled myself forward . . .
and locked it, sobbing in great, choking gasps.

I backed away and waited, holding myself
tightly, feeling my legs buckle.

Staring at the door, I waited for the
pounding to start; for the wood to splinter; for
the first dreadful glimpse of a white porcelain
hand to poke through.

SUNDAY 9:07am

"So let me get this straight," Morgan began again in his usual dry, sarcastic voice. "Your doll came alive last night . . . and tried to attack you."

The way he said it made me think he both believed me *and* thought I was crazy at the same time.

"You think I'm a total nut-bag, right?" I said again, pacing in circles in my room, twisting the phone cord tightly around my finger. "C'mon, Morgan. I'm in serious mental pain here."

"I think you're a total nut-bag . . . but that doesn't mean it didn't happen. Did you tell your mother?"

"Of course. She said it was a bad dream.

As if. Bad dreams don't turn your light off and run across your bedroom floor."

"Or do they?" he said. I could hear the disinterest in his voice, like he was typing while he was talking.

Dreaming. He's one to talk. Morgan Taylor: ace computer fiend, cyber-nerd beyond compare . . . and a newly acquired friend. I met him through his sister, Kelly, the social butterfly. Miss Popularity. I don't have either of them figured out.

Kelly acts all happy and bouncy and chatty all the time, schmoozing from important person to important person all around Fairfield Junior High, as if she's checking off a list, a social quota. She chums up with anybody who is anybody.

She's different when her brother is around. She gets all serious and they talk a lot in hushed whispers. It's like they have a big secret that they can't tell anyone else about. I do know Kelly does an awful lot of running around for Morgan. She's practically at his beck and call, bringing him books and helping him at the library. Weird relationship. In fact, I practically had to fill out a questionnaire before Kelly would even introduce me to him.

There's a reason I called Morgan.

Morgan has this strange hobby I never really paid much attention to before. I heard other kids talk about him but I never really listened much. Actually, I think he scares most other kids. Some say he's a hacker who causes all kinds of trouble on-line, like bringing down phone companies and stuff. Others say they heard he was abducted by aliens and that they did something to his brain. All kinds of dumb rumors. But one thing *is* true . . . Morgan is the guy to go to if you want to know about something weird. All he *does* is collect weird stories and supposedly true accounts of supernatural happenings off the Internet. It's more than a hobby for him. It's an obsession.

"This doll you say came alive, did it actually attack you? Physically?"

"No. Not really. It s-stood up and turned the l-light off. I found it this morning lying on the floor by the bed. I wound up sleeping in the stupid bathroom last night. Morgan, I know how crazy it sounds, but can you help me? Your sister said you'd . . . "

"Okay." He paused for a moment, like he

was thinking about whether or not to help. "Where did you get the doll in the first place?"

I stopped pacing, and stood to watch Mom get in the car. Calvin happily handed her an armful of foil-wrapped serving dishes.

Our aunt, the big caterer, needed last-minute help for a big dinner party and Mom once again said, "Okay." Poor Mom could never say no to Aunt Kathy. This dinner party would be especially grating because Natalie's and Jill's moms were both going to be there . . . *as guests*. Mom would wind up serving Natalie's mom. Boy, did that make her mad.

It took *both* Calvin and me to convince her to let us stay home, but I knew she'd give in. She promised she'd be home by nine.

I watched the car pull out of the driveway, and waved at Mom as Calvin came back inside. "I'm sorry, Morgan. What did you say?"

"Where did you get the doll?"

"Kepler's Toys and Collectibles." I heard a series of clicks and buzzes through the phone from Morgan's end.

"That's the new shop in Fairfield Village Square, right?" he asked.

"Yeah. That's the one."

"Okay. Let me do some checking around and I'll call you back tonight, okay?"

"Okay. Thank you, Morgan. Thank you so much." I already felt better just for telling someone who didn't laugh at me.

"Karen, one other thing. Do you think it's safe keeping the doll? Maybe you should let me send Kelly over to pick it up."

I walked over to the bed and sat down. I couldn't let anyone take that doll away from me now. What could possibly be more rare than a living doll. "Oh, don't worry about the doll. He's not a problem now."

I smiled nervously, drumming my fingers on the top of the securely-locked suitcase, wrapped tightly in bicycle chains.

SUNDAY 7:02pm

I polished every case, dusted every shelf, and completely straightened what would someday be 'The Sanders Toy Exhibition'. My toys stared at me from every corner, from every shelf, from the open closet, and from the open toy box under the window.

I gazed about my room with tired eyes and nervous energy. I couldn't sit still for a moment. The slightest noise would send my pulse into overdrive.

Calvin flew by every now and then, threatening to pilot his Kepler Starcruiser through the vast hostile territories of my room. I would warn him that his ship would encounter my hostile open window. He would hit hyperspace and zoom out of there as fast as he could.

No matter what I tried, my thoughts would drift to the phone, hoping that Morgan would call . . . then to the locked, chained suitcase, hidden in the darkness under my bed.

I marched down the stairs to the kitchen, anxious for some milk to settle my extremely upset stomach.

My mind raced with a million thoughts and possibilities as I opened the refrigerator door.

As the owner of the world's only living doll, I would be famous. I could envision scientific laboratories with hi-tech equipment doing scans and thermograms, television news specials, and magazine articles in every country of the world. *A living doll. Proof of the supernatural.* Friend or foe? How is it possible? What makes it tick? Fame unimagined for me and my one-of-a-kind collectible. The world's only living doll. *Or was it?*

Before I could explore that thought any further, the phone rang, causing me to *jump,* spilling about half a gallon of milk onto the counter.

I quickly grabbed the receiver off the hook

on the kitchen wall. Naturally, the whole phone came down with it. What a pain. Only one stupid screw to hold the thing on. Mom always promises to fix it. "Hello? Sanders residence," I struggled to say.

"Karen? Morgan. I have some information for you."

My heart skipped a beat. "Morgan. What have you found? Is it good?"

"I did some checking around and found some interesting . . . information. Did you check the doll and see where it was manufactured?"

How stupid of me. "No. I didn't think about it . . . and don't ask me to check now." I took a big swallow of milk from my glass and looked out the sliding glass door to the twilight sky.

"Hmmm. Suppose there's some wacko toy manufacturer employee who happens to be really good at voodoo curses. Like in Haiti, Taiwan, or China. Think about it . . . voodoo dolls coming off the assembly line: dresses put on, hair punched in, evil hex placed. A curse in every home."

I spit out my milk, startled by the remark. "You're kidding, right?"

Dead silence from Morgan's end of the

phone. *Was he kidding?*

"Just my own little, creative theory. Okay, then how about a ghostly possession? Several instances of toy inhabitation in upstate New York and the University of Holland. Did anyone own the doll before? Some unhappy kid or a deranged, psycho killer, maybe?"

"No way. Kepler said they were one-of-a-kinds and that we would be the first to own his toys."

"Kepler . . . Wait a minute. *His* toys? These are one-of-a-kind toys? You mean you met the designer?"

"Yeah. A real strange old man. He designed the toys himself and practically gave them to us."

"Hmmm," Morgan trailed off, quieting his voice. He seemed distraught, more so than before. "I did run across a bizarre account of a particular type of poltergeist, reported in Austria and the Netherlands. *A ghast.*"

I heard a faint sound, like a crash. Probably Calvin, tearing around upstairs with his Starcruiser. If he went into my room, I would kill him. "A ghast? What is that?"

Morgan sounded like he was reading to

himself off his screen, barely audible. I had to say I was not very impressed. The more I heard Morgan ramble on about ghosts and voodoo, the dumber I felt. Now I was really wondering if I *had* imagined the whole thing. I probably had nothing more than a stupid doll tied up in that suitcase. More likely, I scared *myself* last night. Yeah. I was taking this thing *way* too seriously.

"Hang on. This report is hard to read. Sorry. It's a rare apparition . . . that can inhabit toys and playthings. Many at once, if it wants to. I don't know what this next part means . . . OH, WAIT! Believed to have carried over a great deal of hatred for children when it died. First reported in the fourteenth century, they supposedly dwelled in straw dolls . . . first causing the owner, usually a young girl, great anguish and terror, and then stealing her away into the night, never to be seen again. It's a good thing you have it locked up . . . this sounds pretty close to what you're . . . Karen?"

I heard a louder crash from upstairs. *Did that come from my room?* "Morgan? Something's going on here. I'll call you back in a minute."

Morgan broke in. "Oh, no. KAREN! Wait a minute. Did you say TOYS earlier? You said

TOYS, not toy, right?"

"Yeah. We bought a bunch. I got a jester and a bear. Jill bought a bunch of dolls. Natalie got a . . ."

Morgan cut me off, sounding frantic. "Wait! Toys! Don't you get it? Where are the other toys? Karen, where are the other toys? Who has the other toys? Are you listening to me? You have to get out of there! NOW!"

A loud crash definitely came from my room. My eyes grew wide as I heard the distinct sound of shelves falling, of cases shattering! A very *real* problem emerged.

Suddenly, all of Morgan's flaky-sounding spook stories faded and I felt *reality* washing back in.

Anger pulsed through my veins, giving me an instant headache to go along with my hyper-tension. *Another loud thump!*

Commander Calvin had just crash landed in the room of the vengeful sister.

I hung up the phone quickly, thoughts of Calvin the Destructor flooding my brain, pushing out all other concerns. After that stunt last night, if he so much as . . .

I lunged up the stairs, two at a time.

I marched down the hall and threw open the door to my room only to find . . . my future lying in shattered, broken, *mauled* pieces on the floor. Not a single toy had been spared. Not from the shelves, the cases, or even the toy box.

Bits of fluff from the insides of stuffed animals floated in the air. Heads, arms, legs, and locks of hair from all of my dolls lay in fragments all over the floor. Every model shattered, every game destroyed, every figure disfigured.

I stood with a slack jaw and tried to

take in the hideous remains of 'The Sanders Toy Exhibition'.

I felt my blood boil, my veins swell, my temples throb. My lips quivered, unable to articulate words.

As I stumbled forward, I kicked the only toy left unbroken. The eight ball.

Tearfully—angrily, I picked it up and shook it, "Am I going to DESTROY the little monster who did this?"

The triangle bobbed in the blue bubbling liquid for a moment and then floated to the top—**It is certain.**

"CALVIN!" I screamed as loudly, as fiercely as I could.

I heard running footsteps thump down the hallway, then Calvin appeared in the doorway, out of breath, MY Kepler bear in his sweaty hand.

"YOU!" I growled. "THIS TIME YOU'VE GONE TOO FAR! YOU SHOULD BE DESTROYED!"

Calvin's eyes darted around the room, his mouth gaping like a fish's. He acted as surprised as I was. "I-I d-don't know what you're talking about! I didn't do this! Why would I destroy your toys? I BOUGHT MOST OF THEM!"

"OH, YEAH?! THEN WHAT ARE YOU DOING WITH MY BEAR?" I yelled, getting right in the little creep's face.

"I WAS GOING TO ASK YOU WHY YOU LEFT IT IN MY ROOM!" Calvin yelled back, pushing his nose an atom's space from mine.

"I-I didn't leave it in your room. I left it in the closet." Bare hangers fell inside the empty closet, as if on cue.

Calvin began blabbering about how much money he had sunk into my toys. About why I would possibly wreck my own toys and blame him, and on and on . . .

I didn't hear much of what he was saying because I was too busy looking at the bear he clutched in his right hand.

The bear's eyes, usually a dark, beady black, began to milk over. A sickly white film began covering them, from *inside*.

Razor-like claws poked from its paws, growing longer by the moment with a soft ripping sound.

Beneath his black, bulbous nose, a handful of sharp, pointed teeth emerged, protruding down at odd angles, like a fistful of sharp nails.

Long strands of drool dripped from its writhing tongue.

It emitted a low growl and began shaking.

10

"CALVIN! LOOK OUT!" I shouted.

Calvin looked down at his hand and screamed as the drooling, snarling mouth of the bear opened wide, ready to bite it in half!

"DROP IT!" I screamed, knocking the bear from Calvin's hand!

Calvin stumbled back into the hall.

I watched as the stuffed bear hit the floor and roared, blinking its bone-white eyes!

In two bounds it vanished under the bed, tossing toy pieces everywhere.

I backed toward the hall . . . listening.

I heard the sound of metal being chewed, of chains clanking, of scraping claws and fangs.

The whole bed shook and trembled, nearly falling apart.

Then I heard a snap.

And the sound of a latch being undone.

"Oh, no. NO! HE LET THE JESTER LOOSE! HE OPENED THE SUITCASE! RUN CALVIN! RUN!" I screamed.

Calvin kicked backward, scooting farther into the hall, whimpering. I tripped over him and fell, staring in horror at the bed.

My heart squeezed tightly in my chest. I stopped breathing and felt my insides twist into a tight knot.

I heard a disgusting little chuckle.

A tiny, white porcelain hand sprang up from the other side of the bed, gripping the top of the blanket. Then another hand . . .

It was him. The jester!

Calvin screamed, "THE BEAR!"

The bear flew out from under the bed and ran straight toward us, its razor claws tearing the carpet to shreds with each lunge!

I saw a rapidly approaching mouth, full of sharp teeth, dripping long strands of foamy drool behind it.

Calvin and I screamed and scrambled toward his room, desperately struggling to get to our feet.

We stumbled across the floor to Calvin's door. The bear's angry growl grew to match the size of its shadow filling the hallway.

I turned and saw Calvin about to slam the door, the bear inches behind! Its mouth opened wide and roared!

SLAM! Calvin closed the door too late!

The bear's head was almost inside the room. The snout pushed and snapped through the opening. Ropy drool smeared the wall as Calvin screamed and pushed against the door with all his might. "HELP! C'MON! IT'S GOING TO EAT US ALIVE!" he screamed.

I slammed against the door, too, and pushed with all my might, my heart pounding like a hammer.

Bumping and jerking in wild motions, we pushed against the door. The stuffed animal's snout caved in slightly, emitting a puff of foam, splitting its seams! It cried and roared, raking the door with its razor claws.

With one final push, we closed it!

And locked it!

I could hear the bear crying and growling, insane with rage, throwing itself against the door again and again . . . using its whole body!

It was as if someone was hurling him against the door.

We slowly backed away, crying out with each splintering thump!

Then I noticed the three red lights moving across the door, just over our heads.

"Uh, Calvin."

"Oh, no," he sobbed.

We both turned and saw it, our brains freezing in horror.

The Kepler starship was floating on its own power, and . . . powering up its lasers.

11

The Kepler starship hovered in the air like an angry hornet. Slowly turning and adjusting for the best possible shot, it seemed.

The three red lights on the door, shining from the lasers, drifted down across our sweat-soaked faces, onto our heaving chests as we backed slowly against the door.

"What do we do? What's it doing?" I squeaked, trying to brace the door with my back.

"It's going to fry us, that's what!" Calvin cried.

The door behind us creaked and buckled as the wild, stuffed bear flung itself against it again and again, growling and snapping furiously!

We swayed to the left, then to the right, the starship angling its bridge to keep the lights trained on our chests.

"We have to do something!" I cried.

A cylindrical pod in the center of the ship began to glow a bright blue. Energy crackled deep inside it, creating a loud whining sound.

"DUCK!" Calvin shouted as the ship fired all three lasers.

Three pencil-thin beams of light hit the door and blew it into a million wooden shards. Calvin and I screamed, covering our heads as the ship dodged the flying debris.

The hideous stuffed bear, knocked back down the hall by the force of the blast, was already recovering—struggling to its padded paws in front of my open bedroom door.

"GO! NOW!" I cried, fleeing into the hall, scrambling past the bear.

The bear shook his head, flinging goo and drool everywhere. His milky-white eyes rolled in their sockets, thin streams of glop running from the edges.

Calvin screamed, scrambling on all fours past the bear who took a careless blind swipe at him as he passed. The razor claws barely missed him, effortlessly carving deep gouges into the wall.

The starship thrust into the hall from

Calvin's room at about eye level and hovered for a moment, scanning for us.

It locked its lasers on us and fired again, blowing a huge chunk off the upstairs hall corner as we fled toward the stairs.

As we lunged to the stairs, we heard the unmistakable sound of claws ripping into the floor, running right behind us.

"THE BANISTER!" Calvin cried, jumping onto it facing forward. I jumped and held on right behind him.

Together, we slid down the rail toward the front door, slipping along at lightning speed.

Above our heads and to the left, we saw the starship shoot out from the upstairs hall and sail down toward the front door as well.

"It's passing us!" Calvin cried, gripping the railing tightly, staring at the post at the bottom of the rail zooming up to meet us.

"JUMP!" I yelled as the starship cut in front of the door and fired straight toward us.

The beams struck the banister, splintering it into a cloud of debris as we fell to the entryway floor.

"The back door! Head for the back door!" I screamed.

We both scrambled for the kitchen and the sliding-glass back door.

The darkness of the kitchen made my heart jump. I distinctly remembered leaving the lights on when I was talking to Morgan.

The sliding glass door was just across the room, in front of us. The floor-length curtain was pulled all the way to the side, revealing our backyard. Cold, blue moonlight cast a rectangle of light onto the tile floor.

Safety! *Or was it?*

"HURRY! We can make it!" Calvin yelled, rushing toward the door.

"WAIT!" I yelped, grabbing Calvin by the shirt. "I saw something."

Across the floor, a small figure stepped from behind the curtain in front of the door.

The figure, barely a foot tall, stepped forward into the rectangle of moonlight coming through the glass.

His pale, porcelain skin glistened. His eyes, pale white at first, began to change, glowing a fierce red. The bell on the end of his hat jingled very softly.

The jester.

Calvin began to cry as the little figure took another step forward in the moonlight, staring at us intently. My stomach lurched. Something about the way the little figure moved seemed unearthly, *unnatural.*

Evil.

The figure began running toward us, his cloth feet pattering rapidly across the kitchen tile. He jerked his arm high over his head. *A gleam.* A knife.

A butcher knife.

"NO! NOOOO!" I screamed as the little figure ran toward us, fast as a freight train, SHRIEKING LOUDLY!

The knife was held high in its stiff hand as it shot straight up to Calvin. In a flash the jester was on top of him! It scrambled up Calvin's shirt and held him by the collar, laughing like a loon.

"CALVIN!" I screamed hysterically. I watched the jester leer into my brother's horrified face. Clutching his shirt, the jester doll raised the knife high in its stiff, cloth arm . . .

Frantically, I grabbed for the nearest thing I could find.

With a loud scream, I pulled the phone

from the wall and smashed it into the jester's tiny face! His porcelain face crunched and shattered under the impact.

I watched as the jester doll became entangled with the curly phone cord as they tumbled through the air, finally smashing onto the floor. The phone receiver bounced high, jerking the limp doll with it.

Behind us, I heard the angry roar of the bear and the soft whine of the starship.

Jerking Calvin along, I shrieked, "C'mon! While we have a chance!"

In a flash, my brother and I ran to the door, opened it, and tore across the backyard as fast as we could possible go.

"He almost killed me! HOLY COW! THAT DOLL ALMOST KILLED ME! I'M NEVER LISTENING TO YOU AGAIN! WAIT! Where are we going?" Calvin called out breathlessly.

"C'MON! We have to get to Jill and Natalie! . . . if it's not already too late."

I swallowed hard, terrible images of my two friends rushing forward in my mind.

SUNDAY 7:40pm

We arrived in Jill's backyard out of breath and still shaking.

Jill's house is very similar to mine. Basically the same floor plan, like most homes in Asbury Estates. Her backyard has a few more trees and a small, covered pontoon boat that her folks take up to Wataga Lake in the summer. Those are about the only differences.

The only light on in the house shone from Jill's bedroom.

We flew across the yard, trying to avoid tripping over the garden hose that snaked its way through the grass.

I knocked on the back door loudly, peering through the glass, sucking in huge gulps of air and clutching my side.

"What if we're too late?" Calvin wheezed.

Then a scream sounded from Jill's open bedroom window.

"C'mon!" I yelled, pulling at the door. It rattled and jerked. Locked!

Another scream from the bedroom window, fainter this time.

Calvin started to wail, sobbing uncontrollably. "HURRY! THEY'RE KILLING HER! THEY'RE KILLING HER!"

I reached under the mat and retrieved the key Jill had told me was there. Calvin waved his arms and urged me on faster. Shaking, I shoved it in the lock and slid the door open. That inky darkness again.

For a moment, a cold dread made me reconsider my actions. What would be waiting for us just inside?

Another scream from upstairs sped us along. We heard soft cries, pleading for whatever was happening to *stop.*

We ducked inside and ran to the stairs.

Everything seemed in order. Nothing unusual, at least not at first glance.

We lunged up the dark stairs, taking

them two at a time.

The light shone from under Jill's bedroom door, exactly where my room is—corner of the upstairs hall.

I looked around nervously. Nothing so far. No bears. No starships. No jesters. Then I remembered what had Jill bought at Kepler's.

Dolls. Old-fashioned dolls with curly hair, cute dresses, and glass eyes that blink.

"Calvin?" I whispered.

"Yeah?"

"Stay close. Very close."

He squeezed my hand. "You don't have to tell me, man. I'm with you."

We eased toward Jill's room. In spite of my anxiousness to save my friend, it would do none of us any good for Calvin and I to get caught as well.

I gripped the doorknob.

"Ready?" I whispered.

Calvin nodded, sweat dripping down his pale, round face.

"GO!" I yelled, turning the doorknob, shoving the door open!

We stumbled inside and SCREAMED, the sight nearly blinding us!

The room could not have looked worse if a grenade had gone off! Jill's bed had been turned over, her desk shattered, her toys smashed and scattered across every inch of the floor.

Then I saw Jill.

She stood near the window, her tear-stained face frozen in fear. Her eyes were glazed over in a look that had lost all hope for rescue. Her arms and legs were being held by at least a dozen dolls. They surrounded her, clutching tightly with their babyish hands. They all had fixed, painted smiles on their porcelain faces. Their mouths opened and closed as if trying to talk, though only sickening gurgles emerged. Their cute dresses were torn and stained with the milky goo that ran from their blinking eyes.

Their eyes had milked over, just like the

bear. My bear.

"JILL! Oh, no! What are they doing to you? What are they? No. OH, NO!" I screeched, staggering backward.

"LOOK! DO YOU SEE IT? LOOK!" Calvin cried out, screaming over the loud rush of wind that whipped through the room.

A tiny doll, barely six inches tall, with straight, brown hair stood in front of Jill, peering up at her, its baby-like arms stretching up.

It seemed like Jill could only move her eyes, so she darted them erratically, rolling them around, trying to take in as much of her situation as she could.

Then she looked straight at me and my blood froze. *I felt Jill's terror.* I could practically hear her fiercely pounding heart.

The tiny doll looked back over its shoulder at me. Its milky eyes blinked slowly and then turned back to face Jill.

A strange, misty light poured from the doll's face, like a search beam from a lighthouse. Jill screamed and shrieked . . . and then started to dissolve. To fade. Her features became waxen, almost doll-like.

With growing horror, I watched as Jill

was being drawn into the light and down into the doll, like a funnel.

Calvin sobbed, releasing my hand.

"CALVIN, NO!" I cried. *I didn't know what to do. Gnawing fear numbed my senses. My reactions. What was happening to Jill? How could we stop it? Were we next?*

Calvin didn't even stop to think about it. He cried out, rushed forward . . . and drop-kicked the little doll with as much might as his small frame could muster.

The little doll sailed past Jill . . . and out the open window.

The dolls holding Jill dropped to the floor, as if their batteries had just died.

The light faded rapidly and the wind died down. Jill wailed, falling to the floor, sucking in air in huge gulps. Her features returned, becoming solid.

We rushed over and helped her up.

"Jill, are you all right? Can you speak? Please be all right," I cried.

"I-I-I'm okay, I think. What? What's going on? It was th-the . . . THE DOLLS! THE DOLLS ARE ALIVE!" Jill started screaming and crying uncontrollably, her legs collapsing, causing her to slump to the floor in a heap.

We did the best we could to calm her quickly. We had to get her out of there! Natalie was still in danger!

"Jill. We have to get out of here! The same thing is probably happening to Natalie!" I said, trying not to yell, putting my arm around her waist and draping her arm over my shoulder. Calvin rushed over to help.

"QUICK! *Call* over there! Warn her fast! USE THE PHONE CORRECTLY!" Calvin shouted, pointing at the phone lying on the floor.

"Good thinking, Calvin!" I grabbed the phone and shakily dialed, peering out the window for any sign of the little, brown-haired doll. Nothing. Just the dark yard.

No answer.

Just a steady series of rings.

"C'mon, Natalie. Pick up the phone! Please! PICK UP THE PHONE!"

Nothing. My heart started hammering again. Flashes of panic surged through me. "She's not answering, Calvin!"

"WELL C'MON! WE HAVE TO GET OVER THERE! NOW!" Calvin shouted, growing angrier by the second.

I heard a muffled crash in the hall, like a table turning over.

"Did you hear that? Calvin? Did you hear that?" I asked, letting the phone drop from my trembling hand.

Calvin nodded, barely able to keep Jill on her feet.

"Jill. Oh, no. Jill! You have more Kepler dolls, don't you?"

I raced past Calvin and Jill and grabbed the bedroom doorknob.

I swung the door open and stumbled back, mouth gaping, eyes widening in terror.

Outside the door, in the darkness of the upstairs hall, stood rows and rows of dolls, all staring forward, milky white eyes blinking in unison. Their tiny, red mouths curled back over shiny, pointed teeth. Their baby-like arms stretched out and all at once . . .

They stepped forward.

14

"C-Calvin, the w-w-window? You think?" My legs felt weak, threatening to go out from beneath me. Staring at the dolls in the hall felt like gazing at rows and rows of marching death.

I backed up slowly, away from the door, as the army of dolls marched forward in the hall, in perfect unison. With each lumbering step, their eyes would grow wide and then blink shut.

Calvin, Jill, and I backed toward the window, watching the dolls with repulsion.

I heard a familiar whining sound.

We stopped.

"Calvin, is th-th-that you?" I asked.

"No. That's not me."

We turned and looked at the window.

The Kepler starship rose slowly into sight outside the window, its three lasers charged up, the snarling stuffed bear holding on tightly underneath!

"RUN!" Calvin cried.

No choice.

We plowed into the hall as the lasers fired, blasting the door to smithereens.

The dolls all gurgled and cooed in delight as we ran into them, wading through the endless marching rows. They followed us with their pupilless eyes and outstretched hands.

I felt a tug and looked down to see a little girl doll with golden, curly hair hitching a ride on my leg. She stared straight up at me and blinked. I screamed as her head raised suddenly and snapped down, her sharp, little teeth planting firmly in my ankle.

"LEAVE ME ALONE!" I shrieked, kicking her off to the side.

"THERE ARE TOO MANY OF THEM!" Calvin screamed, plowing ahead.

We all cried out, sobbing and screeching in pain as they poured over us in waves. I felt their tiny teeth sink into my legs . . . my shins . . . my calves, like red-hot needles. I screamed and pleaded for them to stop, but they just kept coming . . . staring, blinking, *biting*.

I tried to avoid looking down, concentrating instead on the top of the stairs, just down the hall.

We kicked and clawed fiercely, smashing dolls beneath us as we ran, flinging some into the walls, grinding others flat into the floor.

We reached the stairway.

"MADE IT! C'MON!" I cried.

As we grabbed the railing and started down the stairs, most of the dolls stopped.

Some staggered and fell off the top step as if over a waterfall. They bounced down the stairs with us, only to meet a crushing defeat on the floor in the entryway.

"That'll teach you, you little brats!" Calvin shouted, stomping and kicking them until they fell apart.

"CALVIN! FORGET THEM! C'MON!" I shouted, jerking the front door open and dragging Jill behind me.

We flew through the front door and raced into the street, looking desperately over our shoulders for any sign of pursuers.

No one followed.

"Let's get to Natalie's! Hurry!" I cried.

I could only hope we weren't too late.

15

SUNDAY, 7:52pm

We found nothing when we reached Natalie's house. Nothing at all.

We carefully looked through the splintered door frame into her bedroom.

The door lay in broken sections inside the room . . . topping a pile of shattered Darcy™ dream homes, convertibles, spas, supermarkets, wardrobes, and accessories.

Calvin lifted a wooden chunk of the door, peering at the pink mess underneath, like gum stuck under a desk.

He opened his mouth to speak, but I suppose he couldn't think of anything to say.

A strange wind, like the one in Jill's room, must have swept through like a tornado. My eyes drifted from Natalie's bed, overturned onto her desk, to her shelves, which had been ripped from the walls. I stumbled across the pricey contents of her closet, strewn like garbage across the floor. I stopped and picked up a shred of a sweater I once loaned her.

No sign of Natalie anywhere.

Not a trace.

I clutched the shred of cloth tightly. "Th-they . . . they must have . . ."

"Don't even say it," Calvin begged, dropping to his knees, collapsing in exhaustion.

"The dolls . . . The DOLLS! THEY TOOK HER! THEY TOOK HER! LIKE THEY WERE GOING TO TAKE ME!" Jill began sobbing, crying so hard she couldn't breathe. Her eyes stared blankly into space, spilling over with tears. Her whole body trembled.

I staggered around a moment more, staring at the mess, trying to clear my head.

Wincing, I carefully lifted my pant leg. Small bleeding circles of teeth marks covered my ankle and shin. They stung like crazy. Like hornet stings but ten times worse. I felt my stomach churn and knot as I stared at them. I let my pant leg back down, grimacing in pain.

"Karen?" Calvin asked pitifully, staring up at me from the floor. "What are we going to do now?"

What were we going to do? Call the police? They wouldn't believe us. Who would? It sounded too crazy. Living dolls. Marauding stuffed bears. Knife-wielding jesters. They'd lock us away! Sure, they would see the house, the bite marks on us, the splintered doors. They wouldn't know what to believe, but they sure wouldn't believe it was the work of evil, living toys.

Jill was right.

The dolls had taken Natalie.

They had sucked her into a little doll and marched her back to Kepler's Toys and Collectibles. Of that I was certain.

The question: How do we save her?

I knew someone who knew the answer.

"Calvin! Hand me the phone. I have to call Morgan. HURRY!"

16

SUNDAY, 8:13pm

We pedalled our bikes faster and faster, single file down the tree-lined street.

Cars passed by, one or two at a time, their headlights offering brief comfort, security in knowing that other people were around. We couldn't stop them. We couldn't tell them. They wouldn't believe us. Even though we had no way of knowing for sure, I was certain we had to act fast if Natalie was to have any hope of rescue.

I scanned the roadsides and the drainage ditches with worried, anxious eyes, assuming every shadow that moved was a toy, ready to attack.

"Jill? You all right?" I called behind.

"Y-Yes. Let's hurry!" Jill yelled back, trying

to disguise the fear in her voice.

Jill refused to stay behind. Not that I could really blame her. She really didn't want to be left alone. Most of all, Natalie was her friend, too.

"We're almost there. Cut across!" I called, gliding into the empty parking lot of Fairfield Village Square.

The bright blue electric letters shined through the darkness, filling my stomach with sickening dread—Kepler's Toys and Collectibles.

"Calvin?" I called, coasting to a stop in front of the bike racks, the blue letters shining down on my face.

"Yeah?" he replied, pulling quietly up beside me.

"Stay close."

We peered in through the glass doors.

All the lights were off, leaving only the hulking silhouettes of large displays and long, dark aisleways.

Each aisleway could hold a thousand toy assassins.

"You first, man," Calvin whispered, his hands cupped to his eyes as he stared through the glass.

I pushed against the door, expecting it to be locked, or at least an alarm to go off.

It slid silently open.

Like lambs to the slaughter, we stepped into the toy store, huddled together, each of us trembling, darting our eyes around, searching for any sign of movement.

A large, dark shape snaked through the air, drifting from the wall, lowering down toward us. *A long, writhing neck!*

The animatronic brachiosaur.

The dino head moved in closely, its mouth matching its hideous laugh perfectly. The voice sounded different than before.

Mocking, insane laughter.

Its large cartoon eyelids pulled back, revealing milky-white eyeballs with no pupils! Its mouth curled back over pink gums and sharp, dripping teeth.

Its goofy voice rasped, "Howdy there, kids! Welcome to the unhappiest place on earth! We've been expecting you . . . and so has your little friend!"

It pushed in closer, inches from our trembling, terrified bodies.

"And you know what? . . . You're all going to DIE!" The brachiosaur's head broke into hysterical laughter, bouncing violently on the end of its swinging neck!

The neon lights sprang to life all over the store, all along the walls. All the bright colors that seemed so sunny before now seemed garish, harsh . . . blinding.

The high-wire monkeys began chattering overhead. The battery-powered toys in all the bins in the front of the store sprang to life, whirring and clicking and whistling.

We scrambled away from the swinging head of the dinosaur as it gnashed and snapped its jaws in the air.

I stumbled backward into the pile of stuffed animals at the base of the cartoon wishing well.

The stuffed animals. NO!

Alligators. Bears. Gorillas.

A small mountain of stuffed animals waited to break my fall with hundreds of outstretched claws and razor-sharp teeth.

Their eyes were open and white. They growled and snarled, drool dripping from their mouths.

Calvin and Jill both lunged for me.

They barely managed to grab me away from the waiting mound of claws and teeth.

We gasped, startled by a booming voice that shot from the animated cartoon face on the well. Its white eyes opened as a red spotlight fell on its maniacal face.

"You'll find frights and deadly surprises in every aisle! If you need any help, don't hesitate to scream . . . but no one will hear you! NO ONE AT ALL!" The well started laughing, *laughing at us with a hate we could feel! Hate! Just as Morgan had said.*

A ghost was behind this haunting.

A ghost had our friend.

17

We ran past the rows of vacant checkout lines. The numbered lights above each cash register flickered erratically, shooting sparks to all sides.

"What now?" Calvin asked, gripping my hand tightly. "Where do you think Natalie is? Where do we start looking?"

"I'm not sure, Calvin," I yelled. *Good question, though.* Every aisle was a death trap just waiting to happen. Still, what choice did we have? Natalie was trapped in a doll, somewhere in the store.

We had to start searching, but I knew where I wanted to go first. *Sporting goods.*

"C'mon, and stay close. You too, Jill. You with us?"

Jill nodded and pushed closer, horrified

beyond words.

We crept into the sporting goods aisle, slinking near the floor like cats.

Morgan had told me several important things on the phone about our ghast.

Number one. It hates kids. I mean really *hates* them, wanting more than anything for them to suffer. And two, like most ghosts, nothing can really harm it, not in any real, physical sense, anyway.

I picked up a bat, *a big metal one . . .* never one to take words at face value.

"DOWN THERE!" Calvin cried out, pointing toward the aisle across from us—the action figure aisle. "I saw something move!"

"Well, by all means, let's go running down there and see what it is," I said sarcastically. "ARE YOU CRAZY OR SOMETHING? Anything that moves in this place is a trap!"

Then I heard Natalie's voice crying out in anguish from somewhere in the action figure aisle!

Carefully, we snuck down the action figure aisle, heading toward Natalie's voice. Calvin
led the way, knowing the territory the best. His
eyes darted around rapidly, anticipating an
ambush, sweat pouring from his face. The toys
Calvin held so dear were now the fearsome
objects of his terror.

"This isn't right," Calvin whispered.
"These racks were full yesterday."

He pointed at the bare racks and shelves.
The brightly colored packs that once held action
figures now lay empty on the floor beneath us.
The plastic packaging crinkled loudly with each
step.

Calvin gulped, naming off the former
contents of the empty packaging on the ground.
"G.I. Jake™ . . . VirtualNinja Fighters™. . .

CrystalWarriors™ . . . oh, no." He paused at a particularly nasty package. "Punk CyberBikers From Alpha Centauri™."

"Why do I think this is not so good?" I whispered, stopping behind him.

Toward the end of the aisle dozens of boxes were lined up on the floor, stacked one on top of another in low piles, like barriers.

"Help me! Please, someone help me!" Natalie cried again, sounding as if she was in a tremendous amount of pain.

"NATALIE?! WHERE ARE YOU!" I cried out, peering down the dark aisle, searching for any sign of movement from the stacked boxes or among the empty packages.

Suddenly, hundreds of tiny action figures popped up from behind the boxes, using them as barriers, all shouting and training their hi-tech weaponry on us.

I saw G.I. Jakes™ by the dozens. Virtual-Ninja Fighters™! The entire CrystalWarriors™ set! Most fearsome of all, the punked-out Cyber-Bikers™, clutching a Petey the Recording Parrot™ in their True-Grip™ fists.

"Help me! Help me!" Petey™ cried in Natalie's voice.

"It's a trap!" Calvin shouted.

"THEY TRICKED US!" I yelled.

"LET'S GET OUT OF HERE!" Jill screamed, turning to run.

They all fired at once.

Laser beams of different intensities sliced through the air, striking the shelves and the floor. Clouds of smoke and showers of sparks rained down with each explosive impact.

We covered our heads and ran like crazy, the lasers going off all around us. I felt the heat of the beams near my head and hands. Then my throbbing heart stopped as I heard a high-pitched scream . . . and saw Jill fall, sliding forward on the floor, *a smoking hole in her shoulder.*

"NO!" I screamed, grabbing at Jill's arms and pulling her along.

A flurry of laser beams whizzed past Calvin's head. He grabbed a toy laser off the floor and angrily fired back, pulling the trigger rapidly.

Nothing came out.

"It's just a stupid toy!" He shouted, flinging it down the aisle, taking six VirtualNinja Fighters™ down with it.

We ducked out of the aisle, breathing

heavily, watching the barrage of laser fire still exploding beside us.

We pressed ourselves close to the end of the aisle, listening to the tiny shouts and battle cries.

Jill moaned, clutching her shoulder, wincing in pain. "THEY GOT ME! The little creeps got me! Karen, h-how bad is it?" she cried, biting her bottom lip.

I examined the hole in her shirt. A cigarette-size burn graced her shoulder.

"Wow! Does it hurt a lot?" Calvin asked.

Jill's eyes grew wide, crazy. I could tell panic was setting in. "Yeah, you idiot! I just got shot! Of course it hurts!" She started hitting Calvin.

"Hey! Cut it out! You'll live! At least for the moment! More than I can say for Natalie! We have no idea where she is!" Calvin blurted back, fending off her blows.

"BOTH OF YOU, STOP!" I growled.

We all gasped, startled by the sound of a thousand plastic figures clattering on the ground at once.

I peaked around the corner, ready to dodge a laser blast if need be.

The brightly-colored figures lay scattered all over the floor, as if the evil power had left them, turning them back into regular toys.

Great. That means the Ghast was searching for something else to attack us with. Something else to inhabit.

I heard Natalie's voice again.

Weakly crying for help.

And this time, it was no recording.

19

"THIS WAY! HURRY!" I cried, scrambling to my feet and running from the action figure aisle to the one beside it.

Stuffed animals stared stupidly down at us, seemingly normal. No milky eyes. No growing claws. Simply stuffed animals.

Below the furry giraffes, gorillas, and tigers sat shelves full of boxes, brightly colored in a jungle pattern with cellophane windows for looking into . . . *or out of, I thought with a shudder.*

I stopped, listening for the sound of Natalie's voice again. I distinctly heard it in this aisle . . . or was it the aisle over? Calvin and Jill stopped behind me, listening as well.

We stood toward the center of the aisle, back to back, looking around frantically for any sign of movement. The fear between us felt almost tangible, like an invisible chain lashing us together.

I heard a faint sound.

Not a voice, but a rustle.

My eyes widened. My heart beat faster, swelling with dread as I gripped Calvin's hand tightly.

It was the rustle of cellophane.

"Did you hear that?" I asked, the words choking from my tightening throat.

Calvin nodded.

The rustle grew louder.

Definitely cellophane. It sounded exactly like the crinkling rustle of plastic.

Calvin saw it first. Stammering, unable to speak, he pulled his hand away, pointing toward one of the jungle-print boxes near the floor.

I followed the sound of the rustling plastic and Calvin's pointing finger, staring with wide eyes at the box.

Something pressed against the cellophane window . . . *from the inside.*

Then again. The plastic buckled outward and then in again, crackling loudly.

A plastic Tyrannosaurus Rex plunged

through the cellophane window of its box, landing solidly on the floor with glowing red eyes and a terrifying roar!

Jill shrieked loudly as ALL the boxes on the shelves begin shaking, the plastic coverings crinkling and tearing . . . a triceratops horn bursting through . . . a velociraptor claw ripping out.

"Run! RUN! RUUNNNN!" I screamed, flying down the aisle, propelled by a surge of panic.

Our feet pounded the tiles as a stampede of toy dinosaurs followed close behind . . . clawing, biting and snapping at our heels.

20

We fell . . . tripping over each other as we ran, the stampede about to overtake us.

We tumbled and slid across the floor, out of the aisle, into the back wall of the store.

For a brief moment, I saw the door that led to the toy museum and the swinging doors that led to the warehouse.

I turned and saw the toy dinosaurs, crisscrossing their galloping paths, jostling each other in the race toward us, their prey.

Their roars barely overtook our screams. Too late to run! They were coming too fast to escape! *Already I could feel their claws slashing across my stomach, shredding my legs. I could feel their teeth sinking into my head.*

We curled into trembling balls on the floor as the rain of toy reptiles poured over us.

The bat I still carried flew from my hand, rolling to a stop a few feet away.

Shrieking, I waved my hands over my head in a feeble attempt at protection. I swung wildly, knocking away as many of them as I could.

To my surprise, the dinosaurs fell off and slid across the floor like clattering hunks of molded plastic.

I uncurled my body and looked around in disbelief, as did Jill and Calvin.

Like the action figures before, the evil power had fled the toy dinosaurs.

Then I saw why.

Calvin began gasping, unable to breathe, choking out a scream.

What I saw sent waves of stark terror coursing through my body. I started to scoot backward across the floor, unconsciously kicking my legs, my mind screaming to run!

To get away!

About five aisles away, in front of the museum door, *the jester figure stood staring at us, smiling through its cracked mouth.*

21

The jester's face appeared mangled, crushed, hanging in delicate, ceramic pieces beneath his floppy hat. He seemed small compared to the shelves and the racks, but his size could not disguise the power he held.

His eyes glowed a fierce red.

He was overflowing with an evil energy. The seams holding him together swelled and burst, dropping bits of fluff to the floor. He shook violently, as if unable to contain the power inside him. Shafts of light shone from the many holes in his cloth body.

He held a large, gleaming butcher knife in his hand.

"IT'S HIM! THE GHAST IS INSIDE HIM!" I screamed, scrambling to my feet.

The jester ran toward us as fast as a

freight train, the knife held high over his man-gled head, SCREAMING all the while.

This time he would not fail.

This time he would kill us!

Faster and faster he ran. Alarmingly fast, unnaturally fast, his feet scurrying across the tile floor as fast as a spider's.

I grabbed the bat at my feet . . .

The jester lunged, raising the knife high in his stiff hand . . .

I blindly swung the bat with all my strength, the force nearly knocking me back to the floor.

The bat smashed into the jester in mid-air, exploding him into a cloud of fluff and porce-lain fragments.

Calvin and Jill didn't cheer, nor did I.

All we could do was stumble backward, trying not to fall, stunned at the sight.

A ghostly form sprang from the shattered jester. Looming high overhead, its face leered at us, old and skeletal. Milky eyeballs stared from beneath its shimmering hood. A grimace cracked its thinly-veiled mouth. Its arms stretched high as it screamed. Its transparent form seemed to flow in the air, like a jellyfish in water. The air grew dead around it. Icy cold. *It felt like being in the presence of absolute hate.*

"WHOA!" Calvin cried, his mouth a perfect circle, his breath forming a frosty cloud in front of his ashen face.

I shielded my eyes, blinded by the glaring light, numbed by the sensation of its horrifying presence.

The Ghast floated above us.

It lowered its ghostly head and screeched at us with an ear-piercing howl . . .

"SHE'S MINE!" it cried with a voice that froze my blood.

It swirled in the air and flew like a flash into the toy museum.

A girl's scream exploded from that hideous room, tearing my heart in two.

Natalie.

22

We ran into the toy museum, searching for Natalie, unprepared for the shocking sight that greeted us.

The room, at a glance, appeared as it had before. The track lighting shone down on the glass cases. The large, unopened wooden boxes still sat on the dark carpet.

A low, rolling mist began to rise from the floor.

Then I heard the tapping.

Our eyes moved from case to case, listening to the sounds of the tapping on the glass, *coming from the inside of each case.*

The taps grew louder, into a steady pounding.

"The G-Ghost is here," I stammered.

All the collectible Kepler toys had come to

life, clawing and scraping at their cases.

"NATALIE!" I shouted, hoping to hear a cry in return.

Nothing.

Then a low, raspy moan, barely audible over the pounding on the glass.

"Help me, Karen. Help me," the voice groaned.

We ran toward the voice which drifted from a glass case in the far corner of the room.

I tried not to look at the cases as I ran, but I couldn't help it. The steady, violent pounding commanded attention.

Tiny, gleaming fists slammed up into the glass covers over and over again. Milky eyes stared out. Teeth glistened. They wanted out. They wanted out to greet us.

"HURRY PAST! DON'T LOOK! DON'T LOOK IN THE CASES!" I shouted, stifling the screams that swelled in my throat with each resounding blow. Tears ran from my eyes.

"Oh, no. LOOK!" Calvin sobbed, pointing to the corner case, the only one not shaking.

"Natalie . . ." I choked.

There in the glass case, shoved awkwardly onto a sharp wire stand, a Kepler-designed fashion doll stared out at us with horrified eyes. *Human eyes.*

I gasped, feeling my stomach lurch and hollow with dread as the face of the doll changed, dissolved into the ghostly vision of Natalie's face, screaming in pain, real tears pouring from the eyes.

Her tiny mouth moved with a supernatural effort, crying my name.

Red flashes of anger exploded in my brain, making me grip the metal bat tighter.

He had Natalie. Trapped her in a doll. Shoved a wire stand in her back. Had her on display like an oddity.

I howled insanely, an indescribable rage forcing my bat to rise high over my head.

With a bone-chilling cry and tears rolling down my face, I brought the bat down onto the case, shattering the glass into a billion shards. *Poor Natalie fell over with a thud, the wire stand sticking out of her back.*

"I-Is she okay?" Calvin asked, staring with wide eyes.

Jill held her hands to her face, gulping and sobbing, trying not to lose her mind.

I reached carefully through the jagged

teeth of the shattered glass case and plucked my friend out. I cradled her gently, like a baby doll.

The cases in the room all fell silent, a hundred thumps as the toys dropped lifelessly to the cabinet floors. The mist that covered the floor began rolling under the door.

My mind began to clear, the anger giving way to the horror of my situation.

Calvin peered through the window that overlooked the warehouse, sweat rolling down his face.

"The warehouse! Look at the warehouse!" he screamed.

I ran over, clutching Natalie in my hand. Jill followed, her eyes locked onto the doll that held her friend.

"What is it? What . . ." Through the window and the blinds, I saw endless rows of boxes and crates in the warehouse. Hundreds, thousands . . . and the mist spreading on the floor around all of them.

"W-What's going on?" Jill finally asked, mustering her courage, peeking over my shoulder.

The entire warehouse shook and trembled as the toys came to life.

23

Jill stumbled backward, about to faint.

"We have to find Kepler's body, his grave, and FAST!—**He's the GHAST!**" I screamed, grabbing Calvin by the collar, shaking him hard.

"H-H-Hold it! You think I don't know that?" Calvin shouted. "Tell you what, Sparky. Why don't I wait here, while YOU go running around that warehouse?!"

To emphasize his point, Calvin pulled the cord hanging beside him, pulling the blinds up.

Out in the warehouse, dozens of crates and boxes rocked and fell over, crashing off shelves, scooting across the floor . . .

Thousands more followed their lead.

Calvin was right. The warehouse was a death trap now, covered in mist.

Already I could see the lids popping off the

crates, pushed from the inside by slime-covered horns, hands, snouts, and claws. Thousands of milky-white eyes opened and blinked. Hundreds of hunched, dark shadows crept across the concrete floor, growing on the walls.

The warehouse sounded like an angry convention hall.

They were coming for us.

"The boxes! Of course!" I cried, rushing over to the unopened boxes that Kepler had refused to show us before. One was leaning against a case, like an Egyptian sarcophagus, the other lying on the floor like a coffin.

"Calvin! Jill! Help me! I think we just found his grave!"

First, we grabbed the lid of the box lying on the ground. The nails were loose, barely holding it on. "He's in here! He has to be!" I shouted. We pulled the lid off and stared down.

Dozens of smiling jester dolls looked up at us and blinked their pupilless eyes.

We slammed the lid back down with a scream.

"Wrong box," Calvin choked.

The lid flew off, knocking us to the floor. I barely managed to hold on to my Natalie doll.

I looked toward the coffin and screamed, my heart squeezing tightly.

The jesters began peeking out, one after another. Their hats jingled. Their milky eyes blinked, rolling in their sockets. Their little arms and legs kicked and crawled. Then, like insects, they began climbing from the box and plopping to the floor, one after another.

"They're going to kill us! THEY'RE GOING TO KILL US!" Jill screamed, shutting her eyes and kicking frantically, scooting through the shattered glass covering the floor.

The jesters swayed their heads a moment and then ran forward.

In a flash they were all over us, their hands clawing at our clothes—climbing all over us.

Spots exploded in my eyes as I felt the squeezing of my empty lungs, the hands of the jester dolls closing around my throat.

I pulled and tugged frantically at the jesters swarming over me like sewer rats. I could feel them move across me, pulling my hair, scratching my skin, biting my arms and my legs.

I could hear their hideous gurgling and could see silvery strands of drool dripping from their mouths.

Calvin and Jill vanished, rolling under piles of the jester dolls, screaming as if they were on fire.

I staggered forward and . . . *blacked out. Darkness enveloped me, forcing my eyes shut.*

NO! I fought the tremendous weight that pushed at my eyelids. That buckled my knees. That shrouded my brain in a fog.

I moaned and staggered forward, swaying with the weight of my unwelcome guests. I had to reach the other box, the sarcophagus.

I reached it!

My fingers gripped the lid as I watched a jester swing down and sink his teeth into my arm. *It felt like fire.*

I screamed out and yanked the lid off the crate in front of me . . . revealing the mummified corpse of Kepler, the toy designer . . . the Ghast.

I had tried to brace for the sight, suspecting what I would find, but I could not even imagine how horrible he looked.

His eye sockets were choked with cobwebs, his teeth set in a skeletal grin beneath withered yellow skin.

I could not stop staring at the crumbling

face, leering at me from the darkness of the crate. I felt my stomach turn and knot on itself as a cold, numbing fear froze me in place, my nostrils forcing out the horrible stench.

With one final burst of strength, I lunged forward . . . and shoved the Natalie doll into Kepler's withered hands.

All at once, the jesters fell off our bodies, dropping to the floor with a lifeless bounce, their evil energy gone.

With awe, we watched as streams of light drifted from each jester, leaving their bodies with a tug, gathering toward the center of the room, near the ceiling.

Calvin screamed as the warehouse window over his head shattered.

Streams of light poured through, accompanied by an ear-piercing *wail.*

"It's the Ghast!" I screamed. "He's being pulled out of ALL the toys!"

The light swirled near the ceiling like a whirlpool, glowing in bright flashes. Images of all the toys he had possessed dissolved into the twisting vortex.

A low rumble shattered the glass cases around us. Streams of light blasted up from them as well . . . to join the whirlpool.

The Ghast formed, screaming, twisting in the air.

Its arms waved and raked around as though it were trying to swim . . .

Trying to pull away from the funnel of light that was pulling it down . . .

Into the Natalie doll clutched in the skeleton's hands.

"A toy loved by a child," I whispered.

We all watched in shock as the Ghast was sucked into the Natalie doll, screeching in pain!

He squeezed through her eyes, her ears, her mouth, shafts of light escaping in bursts as he entered.

Trapped . . . as he had trapped Natalie.

Natalie.

What about Natalie?

What had I done?

I felt a crushing despair inside as I realized I may have sacrificed my friend. My fault. I *used* her to save our own skins. We came here to save her, but lost her instead. I thought that she would be released when . . .

My fault.

I was about to turn away when Calvin

cried out in alarm, "LOOK! KAREN! LOOK!"

*As the Ghast entered the doll, he was forc-
ing something else out.*

A misty form fell out of the doll, growing
larger, becoming solid . . .

I recognized the form, choking, on hands
and knees, and my heart lept with joy!

My eyes blazed. *Hope.*

"NATALIE!" I cried.

I grabbed her, pulling her back . . .

Barely avoiding the clutching arms of the
Ghast that reached for us, snaking out from the
eyes of the doll . . .

*Before vanishing inside the doll's head
completely.*

Calvin and Jill drew close to the skeleton,
staring at the smoldering doll clutched in its
hands. It still gave off a faint, red glow.

"It's in there," Calvin gasped, reaching
out, but not quite brave enough to touch it.

Natalie and I looked at each other and cried.

*She, because of everything that had hap-
pened. Me, because she was alive.*

SUNDAY, 8:45pm

Hand in hand, we all slowly stumbled through the war-torn remains of Kepler's Toys and Collectibles. Natalie and I walked side by side. It felt great to have her back again. It felt great to be alive.

"Calvin?" I moaned.

"Yeah. What?" he moaned back.

"Remind me to thank Morgan."

"Yeah. Right."

Calvin peered at the mutilated toys lying on the ground like broken shells, shaking his head as we paused at the wishing well in the front of the store.

"What a waste. All those toys," he moaned, wincing and clutching his head.

"I don't want to even *see* a toy, ever again," Natalie mumbled, kicking over a pile of smashed Insectors™.

"I think I'm cured, too. I'm *through* with toys," Jill declared.

"Not me," I said, looking down.

Jill, Natalie, and Calvin all stopped, looking at me as if they couldn't believe what I had just said.

I reached behind my back and revealed what I had hidden . . .

The Kepler fashion doll, burned and mashed. The doll that had trapped Natalie. The doll that now held the horrible Ghast.

Calvin, Jill, and Natalie all shrieked and jumped back, staring at me in disbelief. Amazed that I had even touched the thing, let alone picked it up.

"WHOA! I really don't want to see that thing anywhere near me, all right?" Natalie moaned, holding her fingers up like a cross, as if warding off a vampire.

"You have totally l-lost it, K-Karen," Jill stammered.

I looked down at the doll in my hand.

The smashed face, the burned hair, the

shredded dress. I saw a faint red glow in the eyes, but it didn't scare me anymore. The Ghast was trapped. Hopelessly trapped, if Morgan's information was correct.

"DROP THAT THING! ARE YOU NUTS OR SOMETHING?" Calvin yelled, waving his arms.

"I don't know. Let's see!" I laughed, reaching down, picking a cracked eight ball up from the floor.

"Oh, no," Calvin moaned, slapping his hand to his head.

I shook the eight ball vigorously and smiled, the excitement in my voice barely containable.

"Is this going to be the start of a *very* interesting toy collection?"

The white triangle bobbed around in the blue liquid, catching on the side, but finally freeing itself and floating to the top.

It is certain.

About the Authors

Marty M. Engle and **Johnny Ray Barnes Jr.**, graduates of the Art Institute of Atlanta, are the creators, writers, designers, and illustrators of the **Strange Matter™** series and the **Strange Matter™ World Wide Web page.**

Their interests and expertise range from state-of-the-art 3-D computer graphics and interactive multimedia, to books and scripts (television and motion picture).

Marty lives in La Jolla, California, with his wife Jana and twin terror pets, Polly and Oreo.

Johnny Ray lives in Tierrasanta, California, and spends every free moment with his fiancée, Meredith.

And now an exciting preview of the next

STRANGE MATTER™

#14 Plant People
by Johnny Ray Barnes Jr.

I'm killing it, I thought.

My teeth ground the living thing practically in two, before it got stubborn.

Its flavorless, wet core — *its backbone* — became a stringy mess. I'd have to tug it apart.

I held it tightly in my jaws and pulled with my fist.

SNAP. I tore it apart.

Chomping away, I could only think about one thing: spines. Celery is a vegetable, but it has a spine. I'd read that somewhere, and not in the *National Exclaimer* like my mom teased. I knew it for a fact. Crunching down on the last bits of it in my mouth, I asked myself—*if a vegetable had a spine, could it possibly be alive?*

If so, *I'd just killed it.*

"Bye-bye, appetite," I groaned, and tossed what remained of the stalk to the ground.

I never liked vegetables anyway. Or even meat, for that matter. I'm Rachel Pearson, microwavarian. Canned pasta, boxed fish sticks, nachos with cheese, anything I can heat and eat in five minutes or less.

That *was* my diet. But then I decided to try out for cheerleading. Since then, my mother has been stuffing gardens down my throat.

To make the cheerleading squad, you'll have to be in top shape, Mom says. I'd almost made it through my Saturday afternoon without any vegetables, but then Mom called me to the door and dropped a bunch of celery sticks in my hand. I didn't grumble, though. I just took them, knowing I'd ditch them in the woods . . . *on the way to the new house.*

By "new house", I mean the one being built just behind ours, beyond a small patch of woods that separates its land from ours. It's the first new house to be constructed in my neighborhood in three years. This weekend, while the workers weren't there, would be my best chance to explore it. Mom and Dad have already warned me not to be nosy and to stay away from it, but they don't understand. It's like telling the fish in your aquarium that they can breathe in the water, but don't swim around in it.

When it comes right down to it, I'm not really nosy. Just overly curious. I like to know what's going on in really boring places. Who cares what's going on with the cutest couple in school, or what the class clown did to be sent to the principal's office this time? These are obvious, popular concerns.

I like to dig a little deeper. Like that kid in the back of class who reads a lot and never talks to anyone. *What's he all about?* Or the teacher who disappears from class for the same ten minutes every day. *What's up with that?* Or a house in the middle of being built. *What's it going to look like? Are there any secret rooms?* These are the questions that drive me crazy, and I must have answers.

Clearing the brush, I approached the wooden skeleton that would someday be a home. The bright sunlight gave it almost a feeling of grandeur.

It's almost a shame to finish it, I thought. It's cool the way it is.

A single wide board served as my only bridge to the house. It crossed over a huge trench that circled the foundation. At the bottom of the trench—mud galore. I crossed the board quickly, only feeling it creak once, right in the middle. But I made it, and once inside, I gazed around.

I'm tiny, standing in a house made of matches, I thought, surrounded by the wooden skeleton of the house. Sawdust covered the floors, and empty cola cans and candy wrappers littered the rooms.

"What a fortress of solitude this would make," I told myself, already hoping that somehow the construction would stop and they'd have to leave the house the way it stood.

Then I saw the stairs.

The next level. I had to get there.

Dirty footprints stained each step, forcing me to double-check my nerve. *Construction workers don't work on Saturday do they? Would I get in trouble for trespassing?*

Before I could talk myself out of going any farther, my feet trotted up the stairs to the next floor.

"Hallelujah," I sighed at the top. No one there. I was free to roam in peace.

The entire floor had a warm, yellow glow from the sunlight, and I could look up through the rafters to see Fairfield's blue sky.

Walking over to where a window would

soon be, I found an almost perfect view of the neighborhood, obscured only by the small wooded area I had crossed to get there.

I'd be able to see everything if I could only get a little higher . . .

Now, if my mom could have seen me at that moment, she would have conniption upon conniption. She would say . . . *I shouldn't be at the site. I shouldn't be in the house. I shouldn't climb the rafters . . .*

These imagined scoldings faded away as I scaled the wall frame to its top board. Reaching carefully for the A-shaped supports, I stood up and took in the view through what would soon be a roof.

Awesome. Total freedom. And just as I had suspected, I could see the entire neighborhood. As the birds sang the songs of the day, I took in all of the activity. Sheriff Drake's son, Russell, mowing their lawn. The entire Reece family piling in their car for a day at the YMCA swimming pool. Waylon Burst peeking out of his window across the street from my house . . .

Mom stepping out the back door and calling my name!

"RACHEL!"

My mind screamed for me to duck, so I

did.

She didn't see me, but she wouldn't stop searching. She wouldn't stop calling my name.

Which meant I had to get down and out of here fast.

Just as I lowered my feet to the closest board, *I saw something strange in the woods behind my house.*

Slightly to the right of the path I took to the construction site, something moved.

Something . . . not normal.

It stopped me from moving another inch.

It made me forget about Mom.

In fact, I couldn't even hear the birds singing anymore.

Focusing my attention on the spot, I waited. My joints started hurting from my awkward position, but I wouldn't budge.

You see, things just don't move like this thing moved. There seemed to be too much of it, flowing in and out of the brush.

Curling.

Sneaking.

And there it was again!

This time I saw it clearly. Long, light-colored tentacles moving like snakes, but through the *air*. Large, white spaghetti, spreading out over the entire wooded area until . . .

"RACHEL!"

My mom called out to me again, and the thing stopped moving. Then it pulled its way back into the bushes. Then Mom yelled for the final time . . .

"RACHEL! TESSA'S ON THE PHONE FOR YOU!"

The thing slipped away. It pulled itself through the wooded patch as if it were yanked. Everything grew still again.

Even the birds stayed quiet.

And to my horror, I could see something else down there.

Something moving. Something . . . big.

To get back to my house, *I'd have to walk right past it.*

Wanna read something
frightening?
Something horrifying?
Try reading . . .

DEAD ON ITS TRACKS

Enjoy this special, slithering sample
but beware . . . it's a one way trip!

#12 Dead On Its Tracks

by Johnny Ray Barnes Jr.

1

The morbid anticipation of being afraid, of knowing that unforgettable horrors awaited me just ahead, filled my mind with images of grotesque, man-eating things that promised to haunt my dreams that very night.

But I wouldn't have it any other way.

When I saw a good horror movie, a really good horror movie, I had nightmares. If I made those kind of films, I'd want to give kids bad dreams. It's better than applause. It's better than a good review. It means you really scared them.

That's the effect I hoped "Terror Train" would have on me. The movie, a story of zombies invading a train, had been called the scariest since "Jaws", and I had to see it to believe it. After a week's worth of begging and pleading (a

PG movie that critics said would keep the whole family up nights, even the dog!), Mom and Dad finally gave the nod to let me go.

"Elizabeth, when do I need to pick you up?" Mom asked, turning the corner of Forest Drive, and bringing Fairfield's Gideon 8 Theatres into full view.

"Two hours, Mom," I answered. "You can't ever go wrong with two hours. You're either just a little early or a little late."

"Besides, I don't think her attention span could handle anything much longer than that," my friend, Jacob, smart-mouthed, instantly receiving my elbow in his ribs for his trouble.

"Elizabeth Martin, calm down," Mom commanded as we rolled into the parking lot.

Staying calm was tough when Jacob and I got together. I think his weirdness is contagious. When he's not around, I'm pretty normal. Well, as normal as a football, baseball, basketball-playing girl can be. Everyone calls me a tomboy, except for Jacob. He just says, 'You're scary, man,' then rattles off some kind of story or joke he has dancing in his head. The kids at school think we're a couple, but we're just buddies with a lot in common.

Like horror movies. We both *love* them.

"I hope it's a good one. Nothing's scared me since that blackout a couple of months ago," Jacob admitted.

"Well, I saw an episode of 'Night Gallery' that creeped me out bad. This girl found a monster trapped in a pit, and she began to visit it everyday . . ." My words died off as the car stopped at the front entrance.

"Two hours, then," Mom said as we opened our doors and hopped out. "And be here up front where the lights are. It'll be dark by then."

"No problem-o, Mom-o," I said into the car before shutting the door and bounding over to the ticket window.

Few things are better than going to the movies. Hitting a pitch over the fence, maybe. Or out-running that guy who, for a month, has been teasing you to race him. But other than things like that, there's nothing as rewarding as viewing a movie you've been dying to see on the big screen.

For Jacob and me, Terror Train had been a long time coming. He'd primed me for it, telling me the real-life horror stories the movie had been based on. It sounded too good to miss, and today we'd finally get to see it.

We both dug our money out from our pockets,

walking up that red-carpeted ramp to the ticket window. The usher moved into stub-ripping position. The concession attendant set up two cups in hopes of filling them. The ticket cashier reached above her head, placing something directly over our movie's title on the listing board.

We came to a stop.

No way. No stinking way.

TERROR TRAIN SOLD OUT

Sold out?

NO.

A total and complete injustice.

A stinging slap to the face.

I unsteadily made my way up to the counter, my brows furrowed in confusion.

"Terror Train? Sold out?" I asked.

"Sold out," answered the cashier. "But we still have seats for our seven o'clock show."

"I have a game tonight. I can't make the seven o'clock show," I told her. "Couldn't you let us in? We'll sit in the aisles if we have to."

"Sorry," she said. "It's against fire code regulations."

"This can't be happening . . ." I muttered to myself as Jacob leaned up to the ticket window.

"Can I at least get some mints?" he asked.

Jacob crammed his mouth full of Junior Mints as we walked back out in front of the theatre.

"I guess I'll call my mom to come pick us up, if she's even home yet. This stinks," I griped. "Why couldn't they show it in two theatres?"

"We could always go see another movie," Jacob said, pulling one huge mint made up of ten globbed-together little ones from his candy box. Obviously he had decided to make the best of the situation.

"Forget it. I'm not going to see an action movie. I'm sick of action movies. And I don't want to see one of those stupid cyber-thrillers either," I told him.

Jacob smiled as he chewed the wad of chocolate that was almost too big for his mouth. Behind his eyes, a light bulb glowed brighter with every munch.

"What? What is it?" I asked.

He finished chomping, wiping the excess candy from his lips with the back of his hand.

"Well, do you still want to see something scary?" he asked slyly.

"What are you talking about?" I asked him, giggling just a bit at his serious attitude.

He kept staring at me with his stony expression until I became uneasy, and stopped laughing.

"What is it, Jacob?" I asked again.

Then he cracked a smile.

"I know where we can find something scarier than that movie," he said. "I know where we can find a *real* Terror Train."

THE SCARIEST PLACE IN CYBERSPACE.

Visit STRANGE MATTER™ on the
World Wide Web at
http://www.strangematter.com

for the latest news, fan club information,
contests, cool graphics,
strange downloads and more!

Order now or take this page to your local bookstore!

☐	1-56714-036-X	#1 No Substitutions	$3.50
☐	1-56714-037-8	#2 The Midnight Game	$3.50
☐	1-56714-038-6	#3 Driven to Death	$3.50
☐	1-56714-039-4	#4 A Place to Hide	$3.50
☐	1-56714-040-8	#5 The Last One In	$3.50
☐	1-56714-041-6	#6 Bad Circuits	$3.50
☐	1-56714-042-4	#7 Fly the Unfriendly Skies	$3.50
☐	1-56714-043-2	#8 Frozen Dinners	$3.50
☐	1-56714-044-0	#9 Deadly Delivery	$3.50
☐	1-56714-045-9	#10 Knightmare	$3.50
☐	1-56714-046-7	#11 Something Rotten	$3.50
☐	1-56714-047-5	#12 Dead On Its Tracks	$3.50
☐	1-56714-052-1	#13 Toy Trouble	$3.50
☐	1-56714-053-x	#14 Plant People	$3.50

I'M A STRANGE MATTER™ ZOMBIE!

Please send me the books I have checked above. I am enclosing $ _____ (please add $2.00 to cover shipping and handling). Send check or money order to Montage Publications, 9808 Waples Street, San Diego, California 92121 - no cash or C.O.D.'s please.

NAME _____ AGE _____

ADDRESS _____

CITY _____ STATE _____ ZIP _____

Please allow four to six weeks for delivery. Offer good in the U.S. only. Sorry, mail orders are not available to residents of Canada. Prices subject to change.

ARE YOU A STRANGER?™

If so, get busy and send us your

Cool Drawings

OR

SCARY STORIES

and you may see your work in ...

THE STRANGERS™

N E W S L E T T E R

Send to your fiends at:
STRANGERS ART & STORIES
Montage Publications
9808 Waples St.
San Diego, California 92121

CONTINUE THE ADVENTURE...

with the StrangeMatter™ library.
Experience a terrifying new
StrangeMatter™ adventure every month.

#1 No Substitutions
#2 Midnight Game
#3 Driven to Death
#4 A Place to Hide
#5 The Last One In
#6 Bad Circuits
#7 Fly the Unfriendly Skies

#8 Frozen Dinners
#9 Deadly Delivery
#10 Knightmare
#11 Something Rotten
#12 Dead On Its Tracks
#13 Toy Trouble
#14 Plant People

Available where you buy books.

Coming in January

STRANGERS™

An incredible new club exclusively for readers of Strange Matter™

To receive exclusive information on joining this *strange* new organization, simply fill out the slip below and mail to:

STRANGE MATTER™ INFO •Front Line Art Publishing • 9808 Waples St. • San Diego, California 92121

Name _____ Age _____

Address _____

City _____ State _____ Zip _____

How did you hear about Strange Matter™? _____
_____

What other series do you read? _____
_____

Where did you get this Strange Matter™ book? _____
_____

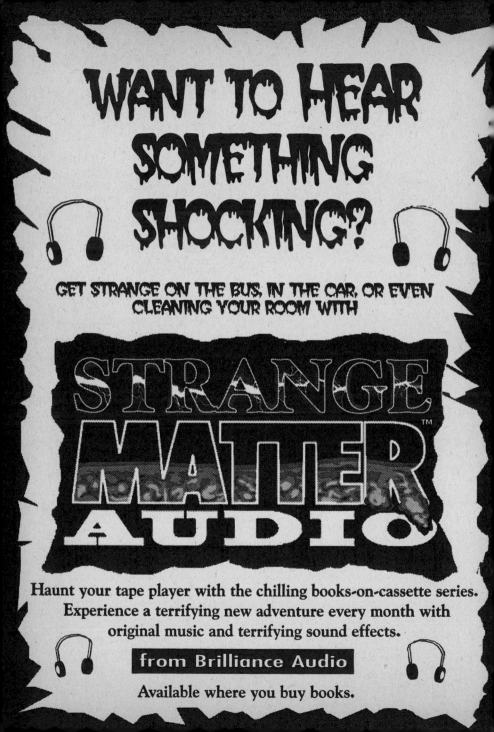

WANT TO HEAR SOMETHING SHOCKING?

GET STRANGE ON THE BUS, IN THE CAR, OR EVEN CLEANING YOUR ROOM WITH

STRANGE MATTER AUDIO™

Haunt your tape player with the chilling books-on-cassette series. Experience a terrifying new adventure every month with original music and terrifying sound effects.

from Brilliance Audio

Available where you buy books.